Love This Life

Theresa Troutman

Love This Life
By
Theresa Troutman

Copyright © 2014 Theresa Troutman

Acknowledgements

Special thanks to my amazing editor, Amy Jackson.
Cover: Cover Designs by James, GoOnWrite.com
This book is dedicated to Melyssa Winchester, who is an
amazing friend, fellow author and brilliant human being. Your
words, kindness, support, and enthusiasm lifts me up and
inspires me. You rock, girlfriend!

Part 1 - Freshman Year of College 1986

Chapter 1 - Home

Sebastian carefully pushed the bedroom door open with his foot while he precariously balanced the wooden tray in his hands. He walked to the bed and smiled. Tess was curled up in a ball, her arm draped over his pillow, sound asleep. He still couldn't believe they were living together, sharing a home, a life. He had never felt such contentment or joy.

"Good morning, beautiful," Sebastian said, sitting down on the edge of the bed.

Tess slowly opened her eyes and spied the breakfast feast that sat on the tray. "Are those Alice's pancakes?" she asked, her spirits lifted even though Sebastian had woken her from a deep sleep. She hated when he did that.

"Yes. Are you hungry?" he asked.

"Yes," she replied, sitting up in bed. "You're going to make me gain ten pounds if you keep cooking like this."

The tray was laid out with a stack of fluffy pancakes on a china plate, flanked by a linen napkin and sterling silver place setting. A single stemmed rose was placed at the top of the tray and there were two glasses of orange juice and coffee.

Sebastian leaned in and kissed her. "I haven't brushed my teeth yet," she protested.

"I don't mind. The first thing I used to do in the morning was smoke a cigarette and drink a cup of coffee."

Tess wrinkled her nose at the thought. "Thank goodness I cured you of that habit."

Sebastian chuckled, sitting on the bed with her. He cut the pancakes and speared a few pieces with the fork and then fed them to Tess.

She actually moaned as she chewed the pancakes, they were so good. "How did you get Alice to give up the recipe?"

"I didn't. She made the batch for me this morning. I did cook them, though."

"I don't think I'd ever give up the secret recipe if I were her."

"Oh, it's not that she won't give up the recipe— the problem is it's not written down," Sebastian explained.

"What?"

"I've watched her makes these things time and time again. She doesn't measure anything. She just throws a dash of this and pinch of that and suddenly, she has pancake batter. Alice says she knows they are ready by the smell."

"Thank you for this." Tess motioned at the breakfast tray. "I love you."

"I love you, too." He took a sip of his coffee and unfolded the Sunday edition of *The New York Times.* Out of habit, he took the crossword section and handed it to Tess. The first section Sebastian went for was Arts and Leisure.

"I think you've brought me breakfast in bed every Sunday since we moved in. You spoil me."

"And I intend to continue to do so to for rest of our lives."

"Even when we have kids and a dog and a cat…?"

"Who said anything about a cat?" Sebastian playfully teased.

"We'll need a bigger bed," Tess mused. She polished off the remaining pancakes and grabbed a pen. Instead of starting the crossword puzzle, she reached for the want ads. One by one, Tess perused the advertisements and began to circle ones she thought might be interesting.

"What are you doing?"

"Looking for a job."

"You don't need a job," Sebastian reiterated. "I promised to take care of you."

"I know, Sebastian, but I need to make some money. I need to start contributing to the house. We have bills to pay, groceries to buy."

"I'll take care of it."

"We've lived here a month already and I keep putting it off. First because we had all the unpacking. Then I relaxed like you asked. Now, I need a job. I need the satisfaction of having my own income. I won't be a kept woman," Tess warned.

"You are the most incredible woman I've ever known. Any girl would jump at the chance to be taken care of."

"And that's why you fell in love with me. I'm not like any other woman you've ever encountered." Tess put down the paper and cuddled into his chest. "Sebastian, this will make me happy and give me a sense of purpose. It will just be a part-time job. Maybe I could work at a bookstore. You never know what kind of contacts I could make there."

Sebastian smiled. "There's my little go-getter. Always looking for the angle to work it to your best advantage."

"Damn right," she smiled back.

"You win! Just promise if the job gets to be too much when classes start, you'll give it up. I know how important NYU is to you. I don't want you stressing over money."

"Deal."

Sebastian and Tess walked down Broadway, past Union Square, until they came upon the Strand Bookstore. He opened the door and Tess entered first. A middle-aged woman wearing wire rimmed glassed greeted them. "Welcome to the Strand."

Tess approached the bookseller and introduced herself. "Hello, I'm Tess Hamilton. I have an interview with the manager."

"Nice to meet you, Tess. If you'll follow me, I'll take you back to the office."

Sebastian kissed her cheek. "I'll be in the art section. Good luck, darling."

As Tess followed the bookseller through the long aisles overflowing with wonderful books, the woman commented, "Charming young man you have there."

Tess chuckled. "Oh, that he is."

In the back corner of the store, there was a tiny office. A glass window gave its occupant a look out onto the sales floor. A woman dressed in a simple, white woven shirt and black pants stood over the desk, paging through a calendar.

The bookseller knocked on the door. She opened it and announced, "Emily, this is Tess Hamilton. She's here for her interview."

Emily walked toward Tess, her hand extended in a greeting. "Nice to meet you. Please have a seat."

Sebastian made himself comfortable in an old, upholstered chair in the corner of the art section. He had amassed a pile of hardcover books after perusing the shelves, and placed them on the floor at his feet. He was reading a book on Andy Warhol when Tess found him twenty minutes later. She smiled, remembering the first time they'd met and he'd tried to seduce her instead of being tutored. He was always intelligent; he just never flaunted it. It was one of the things she loved about him.

"Warhol?" she whispered as she sat down on the arm of the chair.

He looked up at Tess. "When in Rome—" Sebastian closed the book. "Well, shall we celebrate?"

"How do you know I got the job?"

"You're my brilliant fiancée. Of course you got the job. Who wouldn't fall in love with you?"

Tess stood up, her excitement uncontrollable. "I got the job!"

Sebastian gave her hug. "Congratulations, now you can help me put these books back."

Tess playfully punched him in the bicep and grabbed a few books from the pile.

They left the bookstore holding hands. Enjoying the warm July weather as they walked down Broadway, Tess commented, "You know I'd be happy with McDonald's."

"Yes, darling, and you know I'm not taking you to McDonald's to celebrate."

Tess rolled her eyes. There was no point arguing with him over eating establishments. Sebastian took so much pleasure from the simple act of eating, Tess couldn't deny him. "So what did you have in mind?"

"There's a new Italian restaurant that was highly rated in the Zagat Guide. I was reading about it in *The New York Times*." Tess eyed him with suspicion. "It's in the Village, so it's affordable. The decor is casual," he quickly added to dispel her fears.

* * *

"I'm so full, I feel like my seams are going to burst," Tess admitted as they left the restaurant.

"Then I think we should walk off our meal," Sebastian said, taking her hand. "Come with me. There are a few art galleries I want to check out in Chelsea."

They ended up on the corner of Nineteenth and Eighth, where the Fiona Ashford Gallery was located. Once they were inside, Tess walked off to the right while Sebastian veered to the left.

Sebastian stood in front of a painting by Jean-Michel Basquiat, marveling at the bright, intense colors. A woman approached him, saying, "It's a stunning piece."

Sebastian agreed. "I love the suggestive dichotomy of wealth verses poverty."

The woman nodded her head, impressed with his commentary. "I'm Fiona Ashford."

He shook her hand. "Sebastian Irons."

"Are you on holiday, Mr. Irons?" she asked, assuming so due to his accent.

"No, I live here. I'm attending NYU."

"Are you an art major?"

"Undeclared at the moment," Sebastian admitted. "But I've always had a passion for art. When I lived in London I frequently visited the Tate and the Charles Saatchi Gallery. Mr. Saatchi is an amazing person to know if you want to keep up on the latest artists."

"You're friends with Charles Saatchi?"

"He's a family friend. It was always nice to have him around parties so I had someone to talk to."

"So tell me, who does Mr. Saatchi have his eye on these days?"

"Damien Hirst, who's currently attending Goldsmiths College."

"I have a trip to London coming up next month. I'll be sure to investigate Mr. Hirst. Do you like graffiti art as a whole?" Fiona asked, nodding toward the Basquiat.

"I believe art comes in many forms. It would be naïve to think that art only falls into one category. Freedom of expression is what makes an artist. Take Warhol, for instance. He was a commercial artist drawing shoes for Bergdorf Goodman. When he started producing pop art, the critiques laughed and didn't take him seriously. Warhol is brilliant. He realized art can be a business. It can be enjoyed by the masses."

"Unfortunately, the masses can't always afford the price of art," Fiona reminded Sebastian.

"True, but there are always art galleries and museums. Even the poorest of the poor can find beauty in art. It shouldn't be reserved only for the bourgeoisie."

"How would you like to come work with me? I could use someone like you with your unique insight."

Sebastian was taken aback by the suggestion. He hadn't walked into the gallery to find a job, but he had enjoyed his conversation with Ms. Ashford and it was a joy to speak freely regarding his thoughts on art to someone who understood and appreciated it. "Would you be willing to work with my class schedule?"

"Of course. Why don't you stop by tomorrow around eleven and we'll discuss a schedule and salary?"

"Thank you, Ms. Ashford. I look forward to it."

Fiona walked away and Tess rejoined Sebastian. "What was that all about?" she whispered.

"I've just been offered a job here at the gallery," he said with disbelief.

"That's amazing! For a moment I thought you were going to tell me you just bought that painting."

"Do you like the painting?" Sebastian inquired.

"No, sorry, it doesn't appeal to me."

"Well, why don't we walk around the gallery and you can show me what does appeal to you?" Sebastian took her hand and together they viewed the paintings.

Chapter 2 - Absolute Beginners

Sebastian and Tess escaped the subway and climbed the steps at the Eighth Street Station. Tess used her hand to shade her eyes from the sun. "Ugh, I can't believe this is the first day of college and it's eighty degrees. So much for cool, calm, and collected."

Sebastian glanced at her. She was wearing a sleeveless white cotton shirt and a black and white floral skirt. Her hair was pulled back in a high ponytail. "You look fantastic. You have nothing to worry about."

"I'm sweltering."

"I'm sure it will be cooler inside the building," Sebastian reasoned.

"I hope so." She let out a hot breath. "You know where you're going?"

"Got it," he replied, patting his pants pocket containing his schedule. "Meet you for lunch in the cafeteria at twelve thirty?"

"Yes," Tess agreed, leaning in and kissing him on the lips. "I love you."

"I love you, too," he replied.

Tess walked into her first class, which was Government. She took a seat in the front row, eager to hear her professor's lecture. Everyone else who entered the room headed for the back of the lecture hall, leaving Tess all alone. She tapped her pen on the desk with nervous energy.

The professor entered the room. He looked ancient with his short, white hair and slightly bent posture. He wore a tweed jacket and eyeglasses with think black frames that slid down his nose. He reminded Tess of Doctor Magnus Pike from the Thomas Dolby video for *She Blinded Me With Science*. The professor cleared his throat to get the students' attention.

Just then, a late arrival burst through the door. "So nice of you to join us Mr....?"

"Miller," the young man replied.

"Do have a seat Mr. Miller, quickly. And see that you aren't late for my class again."

The young man quickly scanned the room with a grimace, not happy to sit in the front row. He walked over to Tess and sat next to her. The professor began to scribble on the blackboard while Tess turned to observe Mr. Miller.

The first thing Tess noticed was how good-looking he was: strong features, a dimpled chin, brown eyes, and light brown hair. He was wearing khakis and a pale blue polo shirt.

"Man, my brother was right when he warned me about that old coot," he whispered to Tess.

"You were late for class," she reminded him.

"No, I was exactly on time," he countered.

Tess grinned as she shook her head, amused at this guy's carefree attitude. He reminded her of Sebastian, only with an American accent and a smaller budget for his wardrobe.

"I'm Dan, by the way," he introduced, reaching out his hand to shake hers.

"Tess Hamilton," she whispered, hoping the professor wouldn't scold her too.

The professor turned around to lecture the class. Tess dutifully took out her tablet and began to take notes.

Ninety minutes later, Tess packed up her books to go to her next class. "So where are you off to next?" Dan asked, standing from his seat.

"English with Professor Sutton."

"Me, too. We have a half an hour. Want to get some coffee?"

"I don't drink coffee," she said as they walked out of the lecture hall.

"Tea, soda, milk?" he pressed.

"You don't give up, do you?" Tess marveled.

"Nope. Come on, what's the harm?"

"Okay. I could go for a Diet Coke."

"Thank God," Dan sighed with relief. "I need to surround myself with as many smart people as possible."

"What makes you think I'm smart?"

"The smart ones always sit in front, eager to observe and learn," Dan explained.

"You say that like it's a bad thing."

"Oh, not at all. It was a compliment, not an insult."

"Why do you need me? You did get into NYU, after all. They're very selective of who they pick."

Dan laughed. He had the most wonderful laugh. His eyes seemed to twinkle, and laugh lines appeared in the corner of his eyes.

"Please let me in on the joke."

"They're not picky when your mother is one of the esteemed professors and your brother is getting a Master's."

"Wow."

"Yeah, and that leaves me. 'Not the sharpest tool in the shed,' my father would say." Dan held open the door to the cafeteria so Tess could enter first. He poured himself a cup of coffee while Tess grabbed a can of Diet Coke from the cooler. They walked to the cashier and Dan paid for them both before Tess could reach for her wallet.

"Let me pay you," Tess said as they walked to the nearest empty table.

"No need, you can pay next time."

"Thanks." She sat down at the table. "Do you live on campus?"

"No, I commute from Brooklyn. What about you?"

"I commute from New Jersey."

"You're not a native Jersey girl."

"No, I was raised in the suburbs of Philadelphia. My boyfriend has a condo in New Jersey."

"Boyfriend?"

Tess smiled. "Yes, his name is Sebastian."

"That's definitely not a Jersey name for a guy."

"He's English."

"Aw, that explains it. I don't know any Americans named Sebastian."

Tess looked at her wristwatch. "We only have ten minutes until our next class starts. We should get going so you can actually be early."

"What's the fun in that?" he smirked.

Tess stood up from the table. "Suit yourself. I'll save a seat for you in the front row."

Sebastian spotted Tess as she walked through the cafeteria doors at lunchtime. He walked over to her and greeted her with a kiss. They picked up some sandwiches and sat down to eat.

"How has your day been so far?" Sebastian asked as he unwrapped his turkey sandwich.

"Good. I met a guy named Dan Miller. He was late for his first class and had to sit next to me in the front row."

"Really?" Sebastian said with a hint of suspicion.

"You have nothing to be jealous about. I told him I have a boyfriend."

"Oh, that will stop him from putting the moves on you," he said sarcastically.

"Just like you did when we met?"

"I didn't try to pick you up when we first met."

"No, you offered to have sex with me on the library table," Tess reminded.

"I wasn't serious about that. I was simply trying to see if I could rattle you, but you were no-nonsense Hamilton. By the way, that incident happened the second time we met."

"Dan's a nice guy. He's not trying to get me into bed."

"We're on a first name basis, are we?" Sebastian asked with a raised eyebrow.

Tess tried not to laugh, so she covered her mouth with her hand. "Sorry, he doesn't have a title like you, Lord Sebastian."

"I'm not a Lord," he pouted. "That's my brother's title. I'm the honourable Sebastian Andrew Irons, if you must call me by my title."

Tess could no longer hold back and burst into laughter. "That sounds like you should be a judge."

Sebastian shook his head. He was not amused. "English peerage is difficult enough to understand let alone trying to explain it to an American."

Tess reached over and took his hand. "I love you. I don't care what your title is. Now tell me about your day."

"The Language class was a breeze, since I already speak Italian. The Philosophy class was interesting."

"You don't sound very excited," Tess mused.

"Maybe I just need you by my side to stay focused."

"We have a class together this afternoon. I'd be happy to play the part of no-nonsense Hamilton for you."

Sebastian leaned in and whispered in her ear, "You know it turns me on when you act superior and businesslike."

"Maybe later," she replied with a coy wink.

* * *

It had been a good first day at NYU, but Sebastian was happy to be home. The elevator door closed and Sebastian pushed the button to take them to the fourth floor. Sebastian backed Tess into the corner of the elevator and gave her a devilish grin. "I think I'd like to make love to you right here in this lift."

"You'd better hurry up than. We're only going up four floors," she teased.

"I could always push the emergency stop button."

The elevator dinged as they reached their destination. "Too late," she whispered backing out of the lift, motioning him to follow her with a crook of her finger.

Sebastian hurried after Tess. When he caught up, he pushed her up against their front door and claimed her mouth with his. Sebastian fumbled with the key and somehow managed to unlock the front door while his tongue laved the delicate spot on her neck.

They stumbled into the apartment, taking off each other's clothes. They were down to their underwear when Sebastian lifted Tess onto the breakfast bar, spread her legs, and stood between them. "What's gotten into you?" she asked as Sebastian kissed the swell of her breast.

"I've wanted to do this to you all day," he confessed as he worked open the clasp to her white lacy bra. Sebastian slipped it off her shoulders and threw it across the room. He teased her nipple by blowing cool air on it and then he nipped it with his teeth.

Tess sucked in a breath as a spark of excitement shot to her groin. She slipped her hand inside Sebastian's boxers and took hold of his erection. He braced his hands on the counter to stop his knees from giving out. Her touch affected him profoundly. "Lean back," Sebastian ordered.

She did as requested. Sebastian pulled her panties down and touched her, felt she was wet and ready to take his cock. His lips curved up into a smile. "I think you want this as much as I do," he murmured, slipping a finger inside her.

"I want it more," she gasped. "I need to feel you inside me, Sebastian."

Sebastian slipped out of his boxers, kicking them to the floor. He partially slid inside her, pulled out, and on the next thrust buried himself deep inside Tess. "You feel so amazing," he said, closing his eyes and concentrating on the heady sensation.

Tess sat up straight in an effort to get even closer to Sebastian, curling her legs around his waist. They moved in unison, each thrust pushing them closer to the edge. "Just like that," Tess murmured between shallow breaths. And then they reached their climax, clutching onto one another for dear life.

"Oh my God, that was incredible," Sebastian said, kissing her gently on the shoulder.

"We've never had an orgasm at the same time before. How are we supposed to top that?"

"I have no idea," Sebastian chuckled. "Lots of practice, I reckon."

Tess hopped down from the counter and walked over to the kitchen sink. Underneath, she grabbed the Windex and a paper towel. She started cleaning the surface of the counter.

"What are you doing?"

"We just had sex where we eat our breakfast. I have to clean this up."

"Later," Sebastian said, picking her up in his arms and carrying her off to the bedroom.

They lay in bed, Tess in Sebastian's arms, the events of their kitchen encounter playing over in his mind. Talking about this Dan Miller person at lunch had made Sebastian jealous. He didn't know why. He knew Tess loved him, but her reaction to Dan released something primal inside Sebastian. He felt the urge to remind her that he was an amazing lover. He felt the need to brand her as his. Something had shifted and their lovemaking was different. Sebastian wondered if Tess was feeling the same sense of possession he was or had she spent their encounter thinking about Dan Miller.

Chapter 3 - Like To Get To Know You Well

A week after the semester started, Tess and Sebastian were sitting in the cafeteria eating lunch.

"Tomorrow's Friday night, why don't we have dinner and see a show after class?"

"I would love it, but can we afford it?" Tess worried.

"I sold a painting at the gallery this week. My commission will pay for a night on the town," Sebastian explained.

Tess smiled. "I do love going to the theatre with you, and it's been a while since we had a real date night. Let's do it," she agreed.

Sebastian leaned in and kissed her. A shadow fell over them as they realized someone was standing next to their table and they looked up in unison.

"Sorry to interrupt," Dan said, holding his lunch tray.

"Hi," Tess greeted. "Sebastian, this is my classmate, Dan Miller. Dan, this is my boyfriend, Sebastian Irons."

"Fiancé," Sebastian corrected as he shook Dan's hand.

"I didn't know. I guess congratulations are in order."

"Thank you."

"You're welcome to join us," Tess added.

"I can't. I'm meeting some friends for lunch. Thank you for the offer. I just wanted to stop by and say hi."

"Nice to meet you, Dan," Sebastian coolly greeted. "Maybe you can join us some other time."

"Sure." Dan turned to Tess. "I'll see you later."

"Bye." Tess watched as Dan walked across the room and sat down at a table with two male friends. She turned back to Sebastian. "Did you have to be like that?"

"Like what?"

"So smug."

"You didn't tell him we were engaged. I was simply setting the record straight," Sebastian informed her.

"It seemed more like you were marking your territory to me," Tess frowned.

"We are committed to each other. I see no harm in announcing it to your friends." Sebastian was careful how he used his words; he didn't want Tess on his bad side. But damn it, he did feel threatened by Dan Miller, for some reason.

"He could be your friend, too, if you give him a chance. You know, he reminds me a lot of you."

Sebastian rolled his eyes. "I highly doubt that."

"He's charming and just needs someone to believe in his abilities."

"Ability to do what exactly?" He took a deep breath and mentally counted to ten. If Sebastian continued to challenge her, he would likely push her right into Dan Miller's arms. "You're right, Tess. I promise I'll behave better next time."

"Thank you," she said, squeezing his hand.

* * *

Dan Miller squeezed into the lecture hall with a minute to spare. He quickly took a seat next to Tess, and grinned while he opened his text book. "Good morning."

"Good morning."

"Ready for the exam?" he asked in a low voice, leaning into Tess. "Umm, you smell good," he said, closing his eyes and inhaling her perfume.

"It's Yves Saint Laurent, Opium. Sebastian bought it for me," she replied, heat rising in her cheeks.

"Your boyfriend has good taste."

"Yes, he does."

"Class, you'll have sixty minutes to complete the exam. Mr. Miller, put your textbook away, please." The professor passed out the exam papers.

"Busted," Tess teased as she grabbed a sharp number two pencil from her bag.

Forty-five minutes later, Tess finished her exam first. She placed her pencil down on the desktop and snuck a peek at Dan. He was writing away feverishly, his head bent in concentration. She could see that he was almost finished his exam. Their study group must have paid off. Tess felt a sense of accomplishment for being able to help Dan. It was really no different from being a tutor back in high school.

"Pencils down," the professor announced. "Bring your papers to me as you leave."

"Whew, just finished in time," Dan muttered, standing up from the desk. He stretched his arms over his head and Tess caught a glimpse of his taut abs. She quickly turned away to avoid embarrassment.

"How do you think you did on the exam?" Tess asked, refocusing on the business at hand.

"I think I passed. I do have you as my awesome study partner, after all," he replied with a wink. "I need some coffee. Will you join me?"

"Sure."

"So are we still on for our study group tonight?" Dan asked as they walked toward the cafeteria.

"Yes, I can meet you in the library. Sebastian is working at the gallery today so he'll pick me up when he's finished."

The library was packed, so Tess and Dan ended up sharing a table with some fellow students. They all worked diligently, some in groups, some individually. Tess was helping Dan set up an outline for his paper. She whispered tips and tools to use to organize his thoughts. At one point, she reached over to pick up her red pen and her hand brushed against Dan's. He instinctively wrapped his hand around hers, but didn't make eye contact. He looked down at her hand, noticing the naked ring finger. "If you're engaged, why don't you wear a ring?"

"We don't have a lot of money. I didn't want him to spend it on a diamond."

"He dresses like he has a lot of money," Dan observed.

"It's complicated." Tess slowly pulled away. The touch made goosebumps appear on her arm and she nervously rubbed them away. Tess looked at her wristwatch. "It's almost six thirty. Sebastian should be here soon."

"Yeah, I guess I should get going. I know he doesn't like me very much."

Tess wanted to say that it wasn't true, but it was: Sebastian didn't like Dan. She was beginning to wonder if Sebastian had just cause to dislike him. For some reason she couldn't fathom, she was attracted to Dan. It made no sense. Sebastian was amazing and she truly loved him. So why did she get excited and nervous when she was with Dan?

On Saturday morning, Sebastian and Tess were invited to Henry and Alice's condo for breakfast. They ate a scrumptious smorgasbord. Alice went a little overboard with buttermilk pancakes, fluffy scrambled eggs, bacon, and fresh fruit.

Henry and Tess remained at the table sipping their hot beverages while Sebastian and Alice cleaned up the dishes. "Henry, can you give me some advice?" Tess asked quietly.

"Sure, what's on your mind?"

"I've met this guy at NYU. He's really nice and reminds me a lot of Sebastian. We've become friends and study partners, but Sebastian doesn't like him," Tess explained.

"Have you talked to Sebastian about it?"

"I've tried, but he claims Dan has a crush on me and Sebastian doesn't trust him. I feel safe with Dan. He knows Sebastian and I are engaged."

"Do *you* think Dan has a crush on you?"

"Yes," Tess admitted aloud for the first time.

"Do you have crush on him?"

Tess closed her eyes and bowed her head. She took a deep breath and then opened her eyes. "Maybe I do." Tess put her head in the palm of her hands. "Oh, Henry, I'm so confused. I love Sebastian. I want to marry him. How could I possibly have feelings for another guy?"

"Sebastian was the first person you ever dated. Maybe, now that you are at NYU, you're seeing and meeting all types of different people that you wouldn't have come in contact with back in Pennsylvania. This is an exciting time for you. You moved away from home. You and Sebastian are sharing a life together. I know you're a mature young woman, but you must admit, the whole thing has to be a little overwhelming."

What Henry said made perfect sense to Tess. She breathed a sigh of relief to realize that it was okay to feel conflicted, not that it made the situation any easier. "Do you have any suggestions on how to handle these feelings?"

"Honey, I wish I did. Growing up isn't easy. Hell, I'm almost fifty and I don't have life figured out yet. But I will say this: there is nothing like having someone who loves you by your side to navigate this crazy adventure called life."

His statement brought a tear to her eye. Tess stood up from the table and hugged Henry. "Thank you. I'd like to think that if my dad were still alive, he would have said the same thing."

"That is the greatest compliment you could ever give me, Tess."

* * *

Sebastian helped Alice load the dirty dishes into the dishwasher. "Alice, can I ask your advice?"

"Of course, what can I help you with?"

"Tess has this new friend at NYU. He seems charming enough, but something about him just rubs me the wrong way. I think he has a crush on Tess, but I can't convince her of it."

"Charming like you?"

"Yes, that's the problem: I think he reminds me a little too much of me. I know Tess loves me, but what if she becomes attracted to this guy?"

"Why do you doubt yourself and the love you two share?" Alice asked, gently placing her hand on his shoulder.

Sebastian shook his head, a confused expression on his face. "I don't know. I just have this feeling."

"Tess loves you. You have to believe that. You can't let jealousy seep into the relationship. Nothing good can come of that emotion."

Sebastian leaned back on the counter and sighed. "I know you're right, Alice. How do I stop being jealous?"

Alice placed the dish towel on the countertop and gave her full attention to Sebastian. "Show her how much you love her, and I don't mean by spending money on her. Listen to her when she wants to talk. Cook for her. Help her clean. Make her feel secure and safe in the life she chose to live with you."

Sebastian smiled, so grateful for Alice's advice. "You're bloody brilliant, Alice," he said, giving her a hug.

"Yes, I know," Alice joked. "Now get out of here and spend the day with your girl."

* * *

After they left Henry and Alice, Sebastian whisked Tess into the city. They were going to MoMA and then they would meet Sigourney for dinner at the brownstone.

They toured the exhibit—*Vienna 1900: Art, Architecture and Design.* Sebastian enjoyed the paintings of Gustav Klimt, while Tess admired the jewelry and fashion design of the period. "Are you enjoying the exhibit?" Sebastian asked, wrapping his arms around Tess' waist.

"Yes, it reminds me of our time in London." Her heart was happy. Even though the trip to London had occurred under terrible circumstances—Nanny's burial—the trip had cemented Tess and Sebastian's relationship. It was then that Tess agreed to marry Sebastian.

"We should go back soon," Sebastian agreed.

"What do you think about applying for the overseas study program next year? We can go in the spring of our sophomore year."

"To London?"

"It doesn't have to be London. We could go to Rome, Sydney, Paris. We can pick a name out of a hat."

"I can take you on a tour of Europe for our honeymoon and then you can decide which city you like best. Then we can apply." He had promised Tess not to bring up the wedding until December, but it seemed like the perfect opportunity to mention it.

"Not a bad idea," Tess agreed, not wanting to fight with Sebastian. "I'll give it some serious consideration."

Sebastian kissed the crown of her head. "Thank you."

Sebastian opened the front door of Sigourney's brownstone on Park Avenue. Tess entered first, then Sebastian. The sounds of Mozart filled the vestibule. They walked into the sitting room to find Sigourney seated at the piano. She stopped when she noticed her brother and Tess enter the room.

"Hello! I'm so happy you came to visit," Sigourney announced, standing up from the piano and rushing over to give her brother and Tess hugs. "How have you been?"

"Good," Sebastian and Tess said simultaneously.

"Sit down and I'll make us a cocktail," Sigourney said, walking to the drink trolley. She poured Sebastian his usual scotch and popped a bottle of champagne.

"Champagne on a Saturday. What's the occasion?" Sebastian asked.

"Because I feel like it," Sigourney replied, sitting down in the chair opposite her brother.

"So Tess, how is NYU? Do you love it?"

"It's amazing. I love the city. I love the classes. I have a part-time job at the Strand."

"Ooh, they have the most amazing selection of books!" Sigourney agreed. She sat back in the chair and grinned at the couple. "It is so good to see you. It's ridiculous we don't get together more often when you live so close."

"You know it's best this way. If Mother found out you were fraternizing with the enemy, you'd be in a heap of trouble. I won't subject you to that, Sigourney."

"I can take care of Mummy."

"I'd rather you not have to do that," Sebastian remarked.

"How are things at Juilliard?" Tess asked, changing the subject. "You'll graduate this year. What will you do when you finish?"

"I'm not sure yet. I've been thinking of applying to the London Symphony Orchestra and the New York Philharmonic. I love living here in New York, but sometimes I do miss London."

"Tess and I were just talking about studying abroad next year."

"You should do it, Tess. You'll have a natural born tour guide with Sebastian in tow."

"What are we having for dinner?" Sebastian asked. They had skipped lunch and his stomach was beginning to rumble.

"Sushi for you and me, Chinese take-away for Tess." As if on cue, the doorbell rang. "There it is now. Excuse me." Sigourney left the room to answer the door.

They ate, laughed, and played cards after dinner. The grandfather clock chimed nine o'clock. Tess yawned. "We should get going, Sebastian."

"Don't go. I'm having such a good time," Sigourney pleaded. "Spend the night."

Sebastian looked a Tess for her approval. "Okay. I'd like that," Tess agreed.

Sigourney clapped her hands with delight and poured Tess more champagne. They played another round of cards and Tess begged off sleep for one more hour. Finally, at ten o'clock, she hugged Sigourney goodnight.

Sebastian escorted Tess upstairs to the bedroom she had slept in the very first time he had brought her here—only this time, he was sleeping with her. They took off their clothes and crawled into bed naked. Tess curled up in Sebastian's arms. "I had a wonderful day. Thank you."

"You know what the best part is?" he asked, caressing her soft skin. "I don't have to sleep in the bed down the hall."

Tess chuckled at the memory. "That next morning you overslept and I found you naked in bed. I so wanted to climb into bed with you instead of going to the art museum."

"Well, here we are," Sebastian teased, covering her mouth with his. "Please tell me you can stay awake just a little while longer?"

"I think I can be persuaded."

Chapter 4 - To Turn You On

"Tess," Dan called out as he spotted her in the crowded hallway.

Tess turned around and searched the flow of people that streamed by her.

"Good morning," Dan greeted when he finally caught up with her.

At that moment a male student rushed toward them, running down the hall to make a class, and bumped into Dan. He lost his balance and stumbled forward into Tess. Dan's body was pinning hers against the wall.

"Oh," Tess gasped, surprised by the sudden movement, her heart racing.

Dan looked over his shoulder, but the student was out of sight. He looked back at Tess. She held Dan's gaze, her breath labored, their lips just inches apart. "Sorry about that," Dan said.

Tess didn't respond. She stood stone still. The smell of his cologne was intoxicating.

Dan politely moved away from Tess. Straightening his posture, he said very quietly, "I guess we should get to class."

Tess slowly nodded in agreement. She began to walk toward class, but never uttered a word.

Tess sat in the lecture hall next to Dan. The event in the hallway had shaken her. She was excited by the close proximity they shared and her brain wandered. What would it be like to kiss Dan? How could she be attracted to Dan when she was in love with Sebastian? The more she thought about it, the guiltier she felt.

When class ended, Tess stood up from her chair and rushed out of the lecture hall without a word to Dan. Sebastian only had one class that day and then he was heading to the art gallery to work. Maybe it was a good thing for Tess to spend the day alone; she needed to get some fresh air and try to sort out her conflicted feelings.

Pushing open the glass door, she walked out into the crisp fall weather. Instinctively, she wrapped her scarf around her neck and headed to the coffee shop down the street.

It was packed with NYU students. Tess ordered a hot chocolate. When her drink was prepared, she paid the cashier and headed out of the shop, walking toward Washington Square.

The square was bustling with students. It seemed like Tess was never going to find a quiet spot to think. She sat on a park bench, clutching her hot beverage to warm her hands. The next week was Thanksgiving. Where had the time gone? It seemed like only yesterday that Sebastian and Tess were graduating high school. Tess smiled as she thought of Sebastian. He had become the most important person in her world. She loved him; it was as simple as that. Why, then, did she find it hard to concentrate when she was around Dan? Surely, she couldn't be attracted to him while being in love with Sebastian. Maybe it was just infatuation? That must be it, because Tess would never intentionally do something to ruin the relationship she was building with Sebastian.

After her last class, Tess retreated to the library to wait for Sebastian. He was picking her up after his shift at the gallery. She tried to focus on her textbook, but found herself continually reading the same line over and over again, without comprehension.

The shadow of a man cast over her and she looked up, expecting to see Sebastian.

"I've been looking for you all day. Have you been avoiding me?" Dan asked as he took a seat next to her.

"Yes," Tess admitted.

"Why?"

"I needed some time alone to think."

"About what?" a confused Dan asked.

"It's been a long day. Can we talk some other time? Sebastian should be here shortly to pick me up."

"I don't understand. What did I do wrong, Tess?"

Tess loudly exhaled the breath she had been holding in. "You didn't do anything wrong, Dan," she explained, avoiding eye contact.

Dan wouldn't let it go. He lifted her chin with his hand and forced her to make eye contact with him. "You are upset about this morning, when I took you in my arms in the hallway. I didn't mean to do that. That guy pushed me into you."

"I know. Honestly, I'm not upset with you." Tess stood up from the chair, looking for an escape route.

Dan stood up, too. He took a step closer to Tess.

Tess stepped back, trying to keep her distance, but ended up with her back against a bookshelf. She didn't want to be in this position, because as much as she wanted to run away from Dan, she had an equal desire to run to him.

Dan must have sensed her indecision. He took one more step forward. He was so close to her that she could feel his breath on her skin and smell the peppermint in his mouth. He held her gaze as he leaned his forehead against hers. The tips of their noses touched as Dan moved his lips to touch hers. The kiss was slow and tentative at first, then Tess' arms curled around Dan's neck and their kiss deepened.

When Tess returned to her senses, she pushed Dan away. Her trembling hand flew up to cover her mouth, her eyes wide with fear. "This was so wrong," she sputtered. "Don't ever kiss me again."

"You were kissing me back, Tess. Don't deny it. You felt something, too."

"It doesn't matter. I love my fiancé."

"Oh, so now he's your fiancé? Before he was just a boyfriend."

"He was always my fiancé."

* * *

Sebastian headed for the corner of the library, where Tess liked to study. He hadn't seen her since that morning and missed her terribly. As Sebastian turned left and walked down the science aisle, he found Tess embracing another man, kissing him passionately. It was Dan Miller. Sebastian made a hasty retreat from the library, back into the hall, and then sat down on a wooden bench. Taking a few deep breaths, he folded his hands, propped his elbows on his thighs, and rested his forehead on his fists. He forced down the queasy feeling in the pit of his stomach. His eyes must be playing tricks on him. Tess, his fiancée, couldn't have found comfort in another man's arms.

A few minutes later, Tess and Dan walked out into the hall. When she noticed Sebastian, the color drained from her face. She turned to her paramour and said something so softly, Sebastian couldn't make out what it was. He willed himself to remain on the bench. His heart wanted to lunge forward and beat the guy to a pulp. His mind stopped him. Sebastian needed to get the story from Tess. God knows he was no saint, and Tess had forgiven him so many times over the course of their relationship, he owed her this consideration.

Dan took off in the opposite direction. Sebastian stood as Tess cautiously approached him. He resolved not to show any hurt or anger. "Are you ready to go home?" he asked, his voice void of emotion.

Tess nodded, her eyes focused on the floor, avoiding Sebastian's stare. They walked to the subway station in silence. He let Tess board first. She took the last empty seat in the car, while Sebastian stood near the door.

Once they exited the subway station, they made their way on foot to the ferry terminal. On deck, Tess leaned into Sebastian and whispered, "I'm so sorry." Tears were welling up in her eyes, but she quickly blinked them away.

Sebastian acknowledged her with a brief nod of his head. He couldn't do this in public, afraid he would either fly into a rage or break down and cry. Not liking either option, he decided to remain silent.

* * *

They walked through the front door of the condo. Sebastian let out the loud breath that he'd been holding in. He threw his jacket over the back of the kitchen chair and sat down. "Please explain to me what happened. I've spent the last hour going over it again and again in my mind, and I can't sort it out."

He was so calm and in control, Tess wanted to hit him. Wasn't he angry or jealous? Anything would be better than this man with no emotion sitting in front of her. She'd betrayed him and he didn't deserve it. What the hell was wrong with her? She fell to her knees and took his hands. "Just yell at me already. I know I deserve it."

"Do you love him?"

"No!" she cried.

"Okay, I forgive you."

"What?" She was confused by his simple reply. She wiped away the tears with the back of her hand. "I don't understand."

"You were curious about kissing another man. I'm the only one you've ever been with. It makes sense. God knows I had a lot of experience before I settled down with you." He paused for a moment, then quickly added, "But if you'd like me to beat the shit out of that guy, I'd be more than happy to oblige."

Sebastian left her dumbfounded. "I—No, don't beat him up. It's my fault. I let him kiss me." She gaped at him, astonished.

"Did you sleep with him?" The question nagged at the back of his mind and he needed to know.

Tess furiously shook her head back and forth. "No, you're the only one."

"Then it's settled."

"I won't see him again. I promise, Sebastian."

"You have classes with him. You can't make that promise. I'd prefer to trust you won't be tempted to do it again."

Tears began to run down her cheeks once more. "I love you so much. Please, hold me."

Sebastian pulled Tess into his lap and tucked her head under his chin, gently kissing the top of her head. "I love you, too. You're my world. Please don't leave me, I'd be lost without you," he told her, his voice soft and sincere.

Tess sniffled into his chest and then looked up into his eyes. "I can't imagine my world without you, either."

Sebastian removed the handkerchief from the breast pocket of his suit and offered it to Tess. She gratefully accepted and dabbed the tears from her red-rimmed eyes.

"I'll do anything to make this up to you, just name it," Tess said. She looked at Sebastian and tried to read his blank expression. She was at a loss. All she could think to do was kiss him, so she did, pouring all the emotion she felt into it. Sebastian kissed her back. Her heavy heart felt a little lighter. She began pulling on his tie in an attempt to undress him.

Sebastian broke the kiss and gently pushed her back. "No, not tonight. Not like this."

"I don't understand," Tess said in a haze of confusion.

"I love you, Tess, but I won't make love to you when you have another man on your mind." Sebastian brought them both into a standing position. "I'll sleep in the guest bedroom tonight. You have a lot to think about." He kissed her on the cheek and left Tess standing alone in the living room, feeling crestfallen and bewildered.

* * *

Sebastian sat in the guest bed, attempting to read a book. It was to no avail: he couldn't get the image of Tess in Dan's arms out of his mind. Slamming the book closed, Sebastian tossed it on the floor in disgust. Why was Tess attracted to the American? What qualities could Dan possibly possess that would make him a better fit with Tess than Sebastian? He would stand by her and continue to love her, but not physically. Sebastian believed her remorse, but he couldn't bring himself to make love to her tonight. Tess' emotions were still too conflicted and Sebastian felt he had to guard his heart lest she break it into a million tiny little pieces.

There was a light rap on the door. Tess entered without waiting for an invitation. "Can we talk?" she asked quietly, padding toward the bed. She pulled back the navy duvet and climbed into bed with Sebastian.

"It's two in the morning, Tess. Do you really want to do this right now?" Sebastian asked wearily, pushing his fingers through his brown hair.

"I can't sleep without you in our bed," Tess explained.

"Neither can I."

"I'm going to talk to Dan and tell him I'm committed to you and our relationship. I don't know what's gotten into me, but I'm going to make it right."

Sebastian fidgeted under the covers. "Maybe you should explore your feelings for him and have a new experience before we get married."

Tess shook her head in disbelief. "What are you saying, Sebastian?"

"Maybe you should sleep with him; see what you're missing."

Tess gave him an incredulous look. "Excuse me?"

"If you want to have sex with him, then do it."

"Where is this coming from? Earlier tonight you offered to beat Dan up. Now you want me to sleep with him?"

"I still want to pulverize him, Tess. But I've been thinking, you're so naïve when it comes to sexual partners—I'm the only lover you've ever had. Maybe some part of you needs to experience someone different. Maybe that experience will make you realize that we were meant to be together."

"I couldn't cheat on you. You mean too much to me."

"It wouldn't be cheating if I agreed to the liaison."

"You want an open relationship?" Tess all but shouted.

"No, I don't want anyone else but you. You, however, have feelings for this person. I'm worried you'll grow to resent me if you don't explore your feelings for Dan Miller. Years from now, I don't want you to look at me and think, 'Why am I with Sebastian when I had an opportunity to be with Dan?'"

Tess took Sebastian's hand. "Can't we just make love? I want to show you how I feel about you."

Sebastian gave her a melancholy smile. "I can't make love to you right now, because in the back of my mind I'll be wondering if you're thinking of him."

"Ouch, that hurt," she said regarding his stinging comment.

"I'm just being honest. We promised that to each other. Think about what I said. I'll stand by you no matter what decision you make. I love you, Tess."

"Can I at least sleep here with you tonight?" she asked, her head bowed in shame.

"Yes, darling, you can stay here." Sebastian turned out the lamp on the bedside table and lay down. Tess snuggled in close to him, draping her arm over his stomach. Fifteen minutes later, Sebastian felt a change in the rhythm of Tess' breathing and knew she had fallen asleep. He was exhausted, too many thoughts ricocheting around his head. Giving her his blessing to have sex with Dan may have been the stupidest thing he had ever done, but he felt he had no other choice. Ultimately this decision belonged to Tess, and all Sebastian could do was wait for her to decide.

Chapter 5 - Everybody's Got To Learn Sometime

Tess stared at her reflection in the bathroom mirror. There were dark circles under her eyes and her complexion was pale. *You look like hell*, she thought to herself. She attempted to make herself look presentable, applying makeup—heavy on the concealer—and dressing in a new pair of denim jeans, a camel-colored cashmere sweater, and a pair of leather boots. One last glance in the mirror confirmed that she could do little else to help her appearance, so she turned the light off and walked to the kitchen.

Sebastian was taking a bagel out of the toaster. He put cream cheese on it and offered half to Tess.

"I'm not very hungry," she admitted, declining the food.

"Suit yourself," he replied, taking a seat at the counter.

"Are you working today?"

"No, I'm meeting Sigourney for lunch after class." Sebastian took a bite of his bagel and opened *The New York Times.* "What are your plans for today?"

"I don't have any plans. Do you want me to meet you at Sigourney's after my last class?"

"You don't have to come all the way Uptown. I'll meet you at NYU—that way we can get the ferry home," Sebastian explained.

"Okay, let me get my bag and I'm ready to go."

The six-minute ferry ride across the Hudson seemed to take hours. Tess stared out the window, watching the traffic along the Hudson River. Sebastian was nursing a cup of coffee he had brought from home and wasn't particularly chatty. She could hardly blame him. His reaction was such a surprise: first calm acceptance and then his blessing to have an affair. Tess didn't know what to do. A large part of her wanted to run home to her mom and hide in her old bedroom, locking out the world, but she was an adult now and she needed to deal with the situation head-on.

They said their goodbyes in the hallway. Tess kissed Sebastian on the cheek and then turned to the left to go to class. Sebastian walked off in the opposite direction. At least Dan wasn't in her first class that morning—that would give her some time to create a plan of action.

Tess didn't have much of an appetite, so she decided to skip lunch. She made her way to the coffee shop, where she hoped she could sit in silence and read a romance novel. It wasn't her typical genre, but she needed an escape from her own life, even if only temporarily.

It was a good idea—until she practically bumped into someone walking out of the shop. "Sorry, I wasn't paying attention," she mumbled, and then looked up to realize she had come face to face with Dan.

"I've been looking for you. Do you have a moment to talk?"

"Yeah, I guess. Can we go for a walk?"

"Okay," Dan agreed, stepping out of the coffee shop to join Tess on the sidewalk.

They walked together in silence for a few blocks. Finally Dan asked, "Are you okay? Sebastian didn't give you a hard time, did he?"

Tess shook her head. "No, he was surprisingly calm about the whole thing. He saw us kissing in the library."

"I'm sorry, I didn't want to cause a rift between the two of you," Dan apologized.

She stopped walking and turned to face him. "Didn't you? I feel like you've pursued me from the beginning of the semester."

"You were a willing participant."

"Yes, that was my mistake."

"What? That's a ridiculous thing to say. You're nineteen years old—you're not married."

"In my heart I am married to Sebastian. You don't know anything about our relationship."

"You don't seem very happy to me right now," Dan countered.

"I'm not happy. Because I have the most amazing person, who loves me unconditionally, and I had to go and mess it up by allowing myself to be attracted to you!"

"So you admit it: there is something between us."

"Yes, but I'm not willing to throw away my relationship with Sebastian to explore my feelings for you."

"Jesus, you don't pull any punches, do you?" Dan asked, blanching at her bold choice of words.

"I can't see you anymore, Dan. I don't want you sitting next to me in class. I can't be a part of the study group. I need to make a clean break with you to repair my relationship with Sebastian."

"If he's asking you to do that, he's not worth marrying," Dan spat in anger.

Tess laughed. "He's not making me do anything of the sort. He actually encouraged me to have sex with you so I could get it out of my system."

Dan opened his mouth, at a loss for what to say next, then closed it.

"Exactly—there is no response to the generosity my fiancé exudes. I take full responsibility for that kiss and for ending my association with you right now." Tess offered her hand to Dan, but he refused to take it. "Goodbye, Dan."

* * *

Sebastian and Sigourney entered the Russian Tea Room and were promptly seated by the maître d'. After perusing the menus in silence, they ordered their food when the waitress arrived.

"You seem out of sorts today," Sigourney observed after the waitress left the table. "And here I just assumed you wanted me to buy you an expensive meal."

Sebastian would normally have a quick comeback for his sister, but not today. Lack of sleep had left him off his game. "It's Tess."

"What's wrong?"

"I walked in on her kissing another man."

"Our Tess—impossible," Sigourney said, refusing to believe it.

"I wouldn't have believed it if I hadn't witnessed it myself."

"Who was she with?" Sigourney asked, leaning forward, eager for answers.

"This guy she met at NYU. He's in a study group with her." Sebastian took a sip of water. "I'm the only person Tess has ever been with. I understand she might be curious to see what else is out there. I just didn't imagine it would hurt so much."

Sigourney reached out and took her brother's hand. "I'm so sorry. Did you talk to her about your feelings?"

"No, she's feeling guilty enough without me piling on top of it. I told her she should have sex with Dan, to have the experience."

"You what!" Sigourney exclaimed, then remembered her good manners. "Why on earth would you encourage her?"

"Would it have been better if I refused to let her to see him again? If I did that, it would only push her into his arms. I *love* her, Sigourney. I *need* her. My life is worth nothing if Tess isn't a part of it."

"Well, that's a little melodramatic, Sebastian," she said. "But I must admit, you are the best version of yourself when you are with Tess."

"So what do I do now?"

"I don't know if I'm the right person to ask that question. I've never had a long-term relationship."

"Yes, but you're a woman. You must be able to give me some insight into what is going on in Tess' head," Sebastian reasoned.

"Honestly, I have no idea what she must be thinking. You two seem so perfect for each other." The waitress bought a bottle of champagne to the table, opened it, and poured two glasses. "I can talk to her, if you like," Sigourney offered.

"I'm not sure that's the best thing right now. I don't want to pressure her. She needs to make this decision on her own. I won't force her to choose me."

Sigourney looked at her brother, the corner of her mouth turned up in smile. "What happened to my petulant little brother? He's gone and grown up into a mature, selfless young man. I'm so proud of you, Sebastian."

"I didn't invite myself to lunch so you can heap your praise on me," he muttered uncomfortably, lifting the champagne glass to his lips. "Will you come to Thanksgiving dinner next week?"

"I can't, I'm flying back to London. Philomena Cutler-Browne is getting married."

"Who is she marrying?"

"Gordon Lewis-Bishop."

Sebastian began to laugh aloud.

"What is so funny?" Sigourney asked curiously.

"Tess once asked me why so many English people have three names."

"I never really thought about it," Sigourney admitted.

"That's exactly what I told her."

The siblings laughed together. "Tess has got a good head on her shoulders. She'll sort it out and the two of you will get married," Sigourney reassured him.

After lunch, Sigourney bade Sebastian farewell, kissing him on each cheek. She hailed a taxi to make her way Uptown. Sebastian decided to walk down Fifth Avenue: Tess' birthday was the day after Thanksgiving and he had yet to buy her a gift. He wanted to give her the engagement ring he'd purchased six months ago, but never found the right time to present it to her. Under the current circumstances, the timing still wasn't right. He had to come up with something original, romantic, and most importantly, inexpensive. Exactly what that was, he hadn't a clue. He wasn't about to bow out and let Dan Miller win his girl. Sebastian was going to fight.

* * *

Tess was waiting for Sebastian at the Thirty-Ninth Street Terminal. It had been a draining day and all she wanted to do was go back to the condo and relax in a nice hot bubble bath.

Sebastian smiled and greeted her with a quick kiss on the lips. "Hello. How was your day?"

"Better now that you're here," she honestly replied. "How is Sigourney?"

"She's well. I invited her to Thanksgiving dinner next week, but she'll be in London attending a wedding. She sends her regrets."

They boarded the ferry and found two empty seats next to each other. "You look exhausted," Sebastian commented, as he took a seat.

"I am," Tess said, laying her head against Sebastian's shoulder.

"We'll be home soon," he said in a soothing voice.

Tess closed her eyes as she tried to relax in the tub. The smell of lavender candles was meant to calm her mind, but it wasn't working. The radio volume was low. Howard Jones' *No One Is To Blame* played in the background.

Sebastian lightly rapped on the door and opened it just enough to poke his head inside. "I ordered some take-away, if you interested," he announced.

"I'm not hungry."

"Have you eaten anything today?" he asked, walking into the bathroom.

"No."

Sebastian sat on the closed toilet seat next to the tub. "Darling, you have to take care of yourself."

"I'm really stressed right now. I can't think about food." Tess took a deep breath and then continued. "I talked to Dan today. I told him I didn't want to see him anymore. I also left the study group."

"You didn't have to do that for my sake."

"I did it for us, Sebastian. I'm sorry for the pain I've caused you, but I promise I will make it up to you. I swear it."

Sebastian knelt on the tile floor and looked at Tess. She was lovely: her long brown hair pulled back with a hair clip, her pale skin glowing in the candlelight. He pushed a stray strand of hair behind her ear. "Thank you, Tess. It means everything to me that you cherish our relationship so much that you would make those sacrifices."

"Take off your suit. Get in the tub with me. I want to show you how much I love you," Tess pleaded.

"Not tonight," Sebastian whispered. "You need your rest."

The sound of the doorbell ringing caught their attention. "That's the take-away." Sebastian stood and left the bathroom, closing the door behind him.

Chapter 6 - Take A Chance With Me

Sebastian's favorite holiday was Thanksgiving. He loved being surrounded by his make-shift family: Henry, Alice, Tess, and Mrs. Hamilton. Tess and her mom decided to brave New York City for Black Friday shopping deals, which left Sebastian time to prepare for Tess' birthday surprise.

He draped her black Chanel dress on the bed; next to it he laid her La Perla lingerie and silk stockings, and finally the shoebox containing the Manolos. Sebastian placed a note on top of the clothing. It simply said *Wear me*.

He pulled the wrought-iron bistro table from the outside balcony and set it up in the guest bedroom. When the task was completed, he headed out to do the grocery shopping. He would cook in Alice's kitchen so the surprise wouldn't be ruined for Tess.

* * *

"Sebastian, I'm home," Tess called out, closing the condo door. She took off her winter coat and gloves, placing them in the hall closet. The house was quiet. She walked over to the fridge and grabbed a Diet Coke. Then she noticed the handwritten note of the counter and read it.

Be back around 5:00. Love, Sebastian.

She'd had a fun day shopping with her mom in the city, and then she'd dropped Kate off at the train station. Sebastian had something up his sleeve for her birthday, but refused to give her any hints.

Tess gathered the shopping bags and took them into the master bedroom. Inside, she found her clothes laid out on the bed with another note. Why he loved those damned torturous shoes so much, she would never understand. Tess smiled despite the pain she would endure wearing them. Sebastian must have made reservations for a night out in the city. The past few weeks had been rocky for them and she looked forward to date night with her fiancé. Maybe tonight they would finally make love again. This was really the only present Tess wished for. It had been two weeks since they'd last made love, and although Tess had made advances, Sebastian had rebuffed them. She was beginning to wonder if things could ever be the same again after her indiscretion with Dan Miller.

* * *

Sebastian got dressed in Henry and Alice's condo. He stepped out of the bathroom and stood in front of Alice. "What do you think?" He had purchased a new navy suit off the rack at Barney's, and knew it wasn't as nice as the custom-made ones he used to be able to afford.

Alice grinned. "You look very handsome." She straightened his gray striped tie and ran her hands over his lapels. "Tess is going to love it."

"Thank you, Alice. Give me ten minutes and then bring the first course down."

Sebastian walked into the condo to find Tess dressed and ready to go. She was standing in front of the floor-to-ceiling windows overlooking Manhattan, the lights of the city twinkling and bright. He walked up behind her and placed his hands on her shoulders. "Happy birthday, Tess."

Tess turned around to face him. "I like the new suit. You look very dapper."

"You take my breath away," he whispered, leaning in to kiss her. The kiss was quick and sweet. Sebastian took her hand, saying, "Follow me."

He guided Tess to the guest bedroom and opened the door. Inside, the bistro table was dressed with their finest linens, china, silver, and crystal.

"It's just like the efficiency," Tess said, looking over at Sebastian.

"I wanted to re-create the first time I cooked you dinner. I hope you don't mind we're not going out tonight."

Tess threw her arms around his neck. "I love it!"

Sebastian escorted her to the table and pulled out the chair. Tess sat down and quickly unlaced the straps of her shoes, kicking them off under the table. She admired the centerpiece of roses and inhaled the fragrant scent of the blossoms.

He left the room momentarily, and then returned with Alice in tow. She placed salad plates on table. "Sebastian cooked dinner, I'm just helping out for tonight. I hope you enjoy it," she said to Tess.

Tess didn't touch her salad; she simply stared at Sebastian, a single tear of joy escaping her eye. "Thank you so much. This is perfect. You remembered every detail."

Sebastian reached over and took her hand. "You're welcome, darling."

Alice continued to bring course after course to the couple as they enjoyed their dinner. They talked with ease. Sebastian couldn't help but wonder if things were finally getting back to normal.

At the end of the meal, Alice bought a birthday cake to the table. It was six-inch round chocolate cake with buttercream icing. There was one candle on top of the cake, glowing like a beacon.

"If that's all, I think I'll leave you for the evening," Alice said, handing the knife to Tess.

"Thank you, Alice."

Alice winked at them and closed the door as she left the room.

"Make a wish."

Tess closed her eyes, waited a moment, and then blew out the candle. "It's too pretty to eat," she lamented.

"We don't have to eat it right now," Sebastian said, standing up from the table. He offered his hand to Tess, who willingly took it.

Sebastian escorted her into the living room. He walked over to the CD player and hit the play button. Roxy Music's *Avalon* started playing. "Dance with me." He swept Tess up in his arms and moved to the music, swaying to the slow, melodic song. Tess pressed into him, leaning her head on his shoulder.

When the song was over, Sebastian looked at Tess and saw the happiness in her eyes. He felt as if he had recaptured a magic time they had shared long ago. Sebastian raised her hand to his cheek and tenderly kissed her palm. "I love you, Tess."

He felt the time was right, so he got down on one knee, reached into his jacket pocket, and pulled out a red Cartier box. "You're my world. Marry me and I promise I will spend every day for the rest of my life making you happy," Sebastian said, opening the box to reveal a stunning 1/2-carat Asscher cut diamond set in 18-karat gold.

* * *

Tess looked down at Sebastian: his eyes were full of love, his expression full of hope. She honestly hadn't been expecting a proposal, especially in light of their current situation. Tess had gotten her wish. All she wanted was to move forward with Sebastian, and here he was presenting her with the opportunity. She certainly wasn't about to let it slip away. "Yes. All I want is you."

Sebastian stood up and removed the ring from the red box. Tess held out her trembling left hand, and

Sebastian slipped the ring on her finger. It fit perfectly; that didn't surprise Tess at all.

A tear escaped the corner of Sebastian's eye and Tess brushed it away with her thumb. "Don't cry," she begged.

"I'm so happy you said yes," he admitted, feeling simultaneously relieved and elated.

Tess stood on her tiptoes and crushed her lips against his. Sebastian didn't hold back this time; he put all his pent-up emotions into the kiss. It was tender at first, and then it spread like wildfire, hot and eager, setting his heart racing.

Tess pulled away, gasping for air. "Make love to me, Sebastian."

* * *

He wasn't going to say no this time. He had missed her as much as she'd missed him. Sebastian picked Tess up in his arms and carried her into the master bedroom, gently setting her down on her stocking feet. He turned her around and slowly pulled down the zipper on the back of her dress. Tess stepped out of her Chanel and then Sebastian carefully draped it over the chair.

"Lay down on the bed for me," he said as he began taking off his suit in an agonizing, leisurely pace.

Tess watched him, her eyes devouring his nakedness as each layer of clothing was removed.

Sebastian covered her body with his, pushing her arms overhead and holding her still. He kissed her neck and inhaled the scent of her hair. Sebastian had just started his foreplay, but he wanted to dash it all and bury himself inside her. It had been too long since they last made love and his celibate resolve was fading fast.

Sebastian released her arms and slipped off her panties. He pushed between her legs with his knee and she opened up for him. His erection nuzzled against her. She was warm and wet—an invitation to come inside. "I desperately need you," he said in a hoarse voice, his mouth centimeters away from hers.

"What are you waiting for?" she asked in a whisper, lifting her pelvic bone against him. "I need you, too."

That was all Sebastian had to hear. He reached for his cock and positioned it over her opening, sliding inside with ease. He closed his eyes and held his breath, his lips upturned in a smile. She felt amazing. "I've missed you so much."

* * *

Tess held onto Sebastian's arms as he made love to her. This felt so right. How could she ever have contemplated being with another man? Sebastian was her home. He was the only person who could fill her with a myriad of emotions: love, passion, respect, adoration—they were too many to list. He was an amazing lover and she was never going to let him go. Tess vowed to spend the rest of her life proving her love and devotion to Sebastian.

He rolled her onto her side, propped up her leg, and continued to thrust in and out while lying behind her on the bed. His hand slid over her shoulder, down her arm, until he cupped her breast. "That's it—right there," she said in a strained, hushed tone as he pushed her to climax. A few moments later, he followed her over the edge.

Tess turned to face Sebastian and snuggled into him. They were hot and sweaty, trying to catch their breath. Although his face showed no emotion, his eyes were smiling back at her. "I love you, Sebastian."

"Okay," he teased.

She playfully pushed his shoulder, while he kept a tight grip around her waist. Tess looked at the new engagement ring on her finger. It was beautiful and elegant; she couldn't believe it belonged to her. "When did you buy it?" she asked.

"Six months ago," he replied. "Do you like it?"

"It's the most beautiful ring I've ever seen," she admitted. There was no point in arguing over the cost or extravagance of the gift. That was one of the things that made Sebastian—Sebastian.

"I'm glad you like it."

"You have impeccable taste. How could I not like it?"

"Well, yes, that is true," he agreed with a soft chuckle.

"We never got to eat my cake," she bemoaned, changing the subject.

"We can fix that." Sebastian stood up from the bed and walked out of the bedroom.

* * *

Sebastian grabbed a tray from the kitchen. He arranged the birthday cake, two forks, a bottle of champagne, and two flutes on the tray. Walking back into the bedroom carrying the tray, which covered his private parts, he gave her a boyish grin. "Dessert is served."

Tess sat up in bed, propping her back against the pillow. "You didn't bring plates."

"We don't need plates." He popped the cork on the champagne and poured a glass for each of them.

Handing Tess a glass, he joined her in bed. "Happy birthday, darling." Sebastian picked up the fork and dug into the cake. He fed a piece of the delicious confection to Tess.

"This is so good. I'm in heaven," Tess moaned, closing her eyes. She picked up her own fork and continued eating the cake.

Sebastian sat back and gazed at his beautiful fiancée while she ate her birthday cake and drank champagne. A year ago, he could never have predicted things would turn out this way. Time was fleeting and moved at a rapid clip. At last, Tess had accepted his ring—his promise to cherish her forever.

"What are you thinking?"

"I was thinking I have never seen you look more lovely, sitting naked in our bed, eating chocolate cake." He leaned in and kissed her, licking a stray piece of buttercream from her lip.

Chapter 7 - Walk Out To Winter

Sebastian walked in the front door of the condo, holding a package in his hands. "This came from your mother," he announced, setting it on the coffee table.

Tess ripped the tape off the brown corrugated box, eager to see what was inside. She pulled out a white shoe box and removed the lid. She found a dozen old Christmas ornaments along with a handwritten note: *For your first Christmas in your new home. Love, Mom*

"Look at this. These were ornaments from my tree at home when I was growing up."

Sebastian peeked in the box. "There's something else in there," he said, picking up the round tin at the bottom of the box. He opened the tin, inhaling the delicious scent of its contents. "Your mother's chocolate chip cookies." Sebastian took a bite out of one before he offered the remainder of the cookie to Tess.

"I can't believe it's almost Christmas," Tess said.

"There's a lot down the street selling live trees. Maybe next weekend we can buy one," Sebastian suggested.

"Definitely."

Tess was sitting in her Monday morning class, waiting for the lecture to start. Dan squeaked into the room just as the professor turned around to begin his lesson. Late as usual, the only place to sit was in the front row. Tess fiddled with her cuticles, realizing Dan would have to sit next to her. Everything had been going well so far. Dan had kept his distance; they hadn't spoken to one another. She wasn't sure she could handle sitting next to him for ninety minutes, as she felt her heart rate speed up and palms become clammy.

Dan quickly took his seat and quietly opened his notebook. He didn't look her way or speak to her. That was a relief. At least Tess was somewhat able to focus on the lecture and take notes.

At the end of class, Tess packed up her bag and stood to leave the classroom.

It was at that moment Dan chose to speak. "That's some rock you have there," he said, pointing to her ring finger. "So I guess you and Sebastian are officially engaged."

Tess looked down at her sparkling diamond, the light catching the multi-facets of the cut. "Yes, we are."

"Congratulations, Tess, I'm happy for you."

"Thank you. I have to get to my next class." She turned away and then let out a long exhalation. Tess filed out of the lecture hall with her fellow students, leaving Dan Miller behind.

Sebastian was waiting for Tess after her last class. He had just come from working at the gallery. "Hello, darling. How was your day?" he asked, greeting Tess with a kiss on the cheek.

"It was okay." Tess shrugged. "I sat next to Dan Miller in class today."

"And?" Sebastian asked, leery of the response.

"He congratulated us on our engagement."

"That's all?"

"He said he was happy for us."

"Good," he clipped out.

"I don't want to talk about me. How was your day?"

"Did he harass you? Are you sure you're okay?" Sebastian prodded, his mouth pressed into a hard line.

"No, he didn't harass me. We were very civil to one another. It's just that when I see him I feel guilty for hurting you. Kissing him was such a big mistake."

Sebastian gave Tess a hug. "Stop beating yourself up. It's over. We're together. I'm not holding a grudge."

They walked out into the cold December weather and made their way toward the subway station.

Standing on the platform, awaiting the next train, Tess said, "So tell me about your day."

His face lit with enthusiasm. "You'll never guess who walked into the gallery today."

"Who?" New York was a big place and you were bound to bump into someone famous from time to time.

"Andy Warhol."

"That's amazing. Did you get a chance to talk to him?"

"Yes, we talked about his current project with Basquiat."

"You really love working at the gallery, don't you?"

"Yes, can you believe someone like me actually enjoys a job?"

"I told you: when you do something you love, it doesn't feel like a job," Tess responded, lacing her arms through his. "So is Fiona going to show these new paintings?"

"I hope so. She was having dinner with Andy tonight."

"Maybe you'll get all the good gossip next time you work."

The train pulled into the station. The doors opened and a torrent of people escaped the packed car. Sebastian let Tess enter first and followed closely behind her. The doors closed and the train headed Uptown.

* * *

Henry had just helped Sebastian set up the Christmas tree in front of the window, next to the fireplace, when a knock sounded on the door.

Tess ran over and opened it. Two delivery men in navy coveralls stood outside the condo with a tall, thin, wooden crate. "We have a delivery for Sebastian Irons," the one on the left announced.

Sebastian walked up behind Tess. "Please come in," he said, opening the door as wide as possible.

The men came inside and removed the panel on the side of the box with crowbars. They carefully lifted the contents of the box in unison. It was covered with a white canvas work cloth. Carefully, Sebastian removed the cloth to uncover a painting. The painting was large, measuring sixty inches by thirty-six inches. It wasn't a portrait or landscape; it was an abstract painting—just a copper-painted canvas with green splotches. The painting wasn't signed, and Tess had no idea who the artist was. She walked up behind him and they looked at the painting together: Tess wasn't sure what to make of it, while Sebastian beamed with pride.

"I'd like it hung over the fireplace," Sebastian instructed as the two men set to work.

Half an hour later, Sebastian tipped the delivery men before they carted away the wooden crate. The three of them stood in the living room looking at his new acquisition.

Henry and Tess glanced at each other, unsure what to say.

"Well, what do you think?" Sebastian asked.

"I think I could do that if I had a garage and a few cans of paint," Henry joked.

"It looks like they spilled acid on the canvas, yet the canvas is intact. What else would cause that effect?"

"It's from the oxidation series. After the artist painted the canvas, his friends urinated on it. They are also known as the 'piss paintings.'"

"There's more than one? I'm definitely in the wrong line of work," Henry commented in amusement.

Realization dawned on Tess' face as she now understood what she was looking at. She had remembered reading about them in one of Sebastian's art magazines. "Oh my God, how much did that cost?" she whispered, reaching for the armchair to sit down.

"Hope you didn't pay more than a hundred dollars for it," Henry piped in.

"Henry, that's an Andy Warhol painting," Tess informed him.

"The guy who paints soup cans?"

"Yes, the very same guy that paints soup cans," Sebastian confirmed.

Tess became very quiet, so Henry took the hint and left the condo.

"You bought a painting that someone urinated on!" she exclaimed after Henry closed the front door.

"It's probably Victor Hugo's urine, if that makes you feel any better," Sebastian said lightheartedly.

"Victor Hugo is dead," Tess muttered.

Sebastian laughed. "Not the writer Hugo—Halston's lover Hugo."

"Are we going to be able to pay the utilities this month and put food on the table?"

"Yes, darling, you have nothing to worry about. It was an amazing deal. I couldn't pass it up. I didn't even have to get Mr. Hume's okay to purchase the painting."

"Wonderful, that only means it cost less than thirty thousand dollars."

"Yes, it was less than thirty-thousand." He declined telling her the price tag was just *under* thirty thousand dollars.

Sebastian was overjoyed, like a child getting the best Christmas present ever. Tess couldn't scold him for making the decision without her input—it was his money, after all. "Well, the colors are pretty," she finally conceded.

"Art is always a good investment. I promise this will put the kids through college one day," Sebastian reassured, placing his arm around Tess. "Until that time comes, I'm going to enjoy it. It fits the spot perfectly, don't you think?"

"Yes, it does," Tess agreed.

The doorbell rang again. Tess actually groaned aloud. "Let me guess, that's the Jackson Pollack."

"They would complement each other," Sebastian mused, "but it's just the Chinese take-away."

"Thank God," she grumbled under her breath as Sebastian opened the door and paid for the food.

After they ate dinner, they began to decorate the Christmas tree, using the heirlooms Tess' mom had sent and some new ornaments Sebastian and Tess had bought together.

"You know, this is the first time I've ever decorated a tree."

Tess looked at him with skepticism. "What are you talking about? You never had a tree growing up?"

"We always had a tree, but the servants decorated it."

Tess shook her head. "I can't imagine growing up like that."

"Lily never wanted us getting dirty doing menial tasks."

"Unbelievable," Tess said, shaking her head. "Are you having fun doing this with me?"

"Very much so," he confirmed, carefully hanging a glass ornament on an evergreen bough.

They stood back and admired their work. "It's beautiful," Tess said.

The fire crackled and hissed as it burned in the fireplace. The white lights twinkled on the Christmas tree as the smell of the evergreen diffused through the living room. Sebastian took Tess in his arms and held her tight. This was all he'd ever wanted—well, almost.

"Tess, do you know what the best Christmas present would be?"

"What?"

"Setting a date for the wedding."

Tess looked up at Sebastian. This time she had no qualms or hesitations. "Okay, let's set a date," she agreed.

Sebastian picked her up off the floor and spun around in a circle, planting little kisses all over her face. Tess giggled as he gently returned her to the floor, slightly dizzy from the spinning.

"May twenty-seventh and then a honeymoon trip to Europe—please say yes."

She didn't understand his fixation with the date, but she willingly surrendered. "I'll do it if you promise not to buy me a Christmas present this year. We'll save the money for Europe."

"Deal," he agreed, leaning in for a proper slow, romantic kiss.

Tess pulled away and opened her eyes. "I have one more request."

"Name it."

"I want to get married right here in the condo, with Manhattan as our backdrop."

"You don't have to be frugal. We can have the wedding anywhere," Sebastian reassured.

"I want it here—in the place I love, with the people I love. We'll keep it small and intimate: just you and me, Henry and Alice, Mom, and Sigourney."

Sebastian pondered her request. The city would certainly be a magnificent altar. He wasn't a religious man, so a church seemed a bit over the top, even by his standards. It was the perfect solution. "I think it's a brilliant idea. Let's do it."

Sebastian and Tess hosted Christmas Eve dinner at their condo. They were joined by Henry, Alice, Sigourney, and Kate.

"I love the tree," Tess' mom said in admiration.

"It was so thoughtful of you to send Tess the ornaments. I'm really glad you were able to come tonight. Tess would have been miserable if you weren't here," Sebastian said.

"Dinner is ready," Tess called from the kitchen.

Everyone took their seats at the table. "Before we start, I want to thank you all from coming this evening. Tess and I are so happy to spend the holiday with you in our new home."

Everyone raised their glass to toast. "I'd also like to take this opportunity to announce that Tess and I have set a wedding date for May twenty-seventh."

Sigourney let out an audible gasp. "That's only five months away. How can I book The Plaza on such short notice?"

Sebastian chuckled, but everyone else remained silent. "We're having the wedding here at the condo and we want to invite all of you."

Sigourney looked at Tess, an alarmed expression on her face.

"It was my suggestion, Sigourney. What could be better than getting married with Manhattan as our backdrop?" Tess asked.

"I think it's a wonderful idea," Kate said, placing her hand on top of Tess'.

"To Sebastian and Tess," Henry announced, raising his glass.

The group enjoyed their meal, sharing conversation and laughter. After dessert, they retreated to the living room where they opened gifts while Christmas music played on the stereo.

Tess and her mom were taking empty glasses to the kitchen when Sigourney cornered them. "Tess, you have to allow me to take you shopping for your wedding dress. Kate, you must come along."

"Sigourney, it will have to be an off-the-rack dress—it's all I can afford."

Sebastian's sister gave a little pout. "I was going to take you to Saks. They have an amazing bridal salon. We can make a day of it. What do you say?"

Tess looked at her mom, who gave a brief nod, and then caved to Sigourney's request. "Fine, but that doesn't mean I'll be buying a dress. We're just looking, right?"

"Absolutely!" Sigourney agreed, clapped her hands with delight.

Later, after everyone had gone home for the evening, Sebastian and Tess lay in bed together.

"That went well, don't you think?" Sebastian asked.

"It was a nice evening, although Sigourney cornered and begged me to let her take me shopping for a wedding dress."

"Oh, goody," he razzed.

"You have to talk to her, Sebastian."

"Let her have her fun. God knows when she'll ever get around to getting married. Go try on some pretty dresses with her. Who knows? You might just find the perfect one."

"I guess there's no harm in looking," Tess agreed. She reached over to the bedside table and turned off the light. Nuzzling into Sebastian's arms she whispered, "Merry Christmas."

Chapter 8 - Dress You Up

Tess and her mom met up with Sigourney outside Saks Fifth Avenue. Sigourney was wearing a fur coat and leather pumps, while Tess and her mom were dressed in simple cotton skirts and blouses.

"Hello! I'm so excited," she announced, hugging Tess.

Tess was filled with doubt: she knew her future sister-in-law meant well with her offer to help her shop for her wedding gown, but she dreaded the consequences. If Sigourney was half the shopper Sebastian was, it would be an expensive shopping trip.

The three ladies entered the department store and took the elevator to the bridal salon. Sigourney had set up an appointment with a bridal consultant, so she walked over to the desk to chat with the woman.

Tess' mom smiled as she looked upon the dressed mannequins. "I can't wait to see you try these on," she told her daughter.

"Mom, we can't afford this," Tess fretted.

"I have some money tucked away for the wedding. Since we don't need to find a venue for the reception, I want you to use the money to buy the dress."

Sigourney and the consultant joined them. "Welcome to Saks. Are you ready to find the perfect dress?"

Tess gave an apprehensive smile. "I guess so."

"What style do you like?" the consultant asked, trying to determine where to start their hunt.

"I want something, simple and elegant—nothing big and puffy," Tess managed to say. It was the '80s and everything seemed big and puffy as Tess looked around the showroom.

"What about something by Armani or Calvin Klein?" Sigourney suggested. "Something with sleek lines."

The consultant nodded. "Follow me." She escorted the ladies into a private sitting room and offered them beverages. Sigourney joined the consultant in the storeroom.

"You might think Sigourney was getting married. She's so excited about this," Tess whispered to her mom as they sat on the blue silk tufted settee and awaited their return.

"I think it's sweet she wants to help. I'm so glad she and Sebastian maintained their relationship after what happened between him and his mother."

"I know. I guess I just always envisioned you and me going to the Bridal Shop back home when it came time for me to get married."

The consultant and Sigourney returned, each holding two dresses. "I brought these out to see if any of the styles appeal to you," the consultant began. "First, we have a Calvin Klein silk." She held it up to Tess to examine. It looked like a slip—flimsy white fabric with spaghetti straps. It certainly was simple and sleek, but Tess couldn't see herself looking very good in it. She was only five-foot two and had curves. The dress was wrong for her body type.

"Not that one," Tess said.

"Next, we have Ralph Lauren." The consultant held up the white cotton dress. It had a country feel to it, with long sleeves and a high-neck lace collar. It looked like something a cowboy's wife would wear.

"Sorry, I don't care for that one, either."

"How about this one," Sigourney jumped in, "it's Armani." The gown was white satin with an ornate beaded bodice and short sleeves, and a long column skirt.

"You're getting better," Tess admitted. "Let's see the last one."

"The last one is Diane von Furstenberg," the consultant explained as Sigourney held it up for inspection. It was a variation on the wrap dress—white jersey with a fabric belt, plunging neckline, and long sleeves.

"The neckline is too low," Tess stated, although she did like the style of the dress.

"We can always alter it," the consultant explained. "Why don't you come back with me and we'll try these two on?"

Tess stood in the dressing room while the consultant pulled, prodded, and pinned her into the dress. The Armani, while beautiful, was just too over-the-top for their simple wedding. The von Furstenberg, while simple, was too sexy. She tried on a few more gowns after that and played fashion show for her mom and Sigourney. After an hour and a half, she was no closer to finding a gown than she had been when they first walked through the doors. Tess was getting cranky and hungry and just wanted to get back into her own clothes.

They left the bridal salon and had lunch at the café in Saks. The food made Tess feel better. "I appreciate that you made the appointment, Sigourney. I'm sorry I couldn't find anything I liked today."

"No worries. We can always try Bergdorf's or Bloomingdale's," she replied, unfazed.

"I don't think I'm up for that today," Tess admitted.

"Then we'll just window shop. Kate did make the trek into the city. We can't end the day so early."

"I'd like that," Kate agreed.

Tess was overruled, so she tried to take it in stride and enjoy the day. Maybe in a few weeks she could quietly head back to Pennsylvania and go to the little bridal salon with her mom and find a two-hundred-dollar dress to suit her taste.

They walked along the couture floor, passing Dior, Yamamoto, and Céline. Tess couldn't help herself and stopped outside the Chanel shop. In the window there was a mannequin dressed in a floor-length gown in the palest pink color—it was almost nude. The skirt was tulle, simple and flowing. The bodice was silk with a sweetheart neckline. The short sleeves were beaded with white seed pearls.

Sigourney and Kate continued to walk down the aisle, deep in conversation, not noticing that Tess had stopped. When they did, they doubled back.

"It's the most beautiful dress I've ever seen," Tess breathlessly stated, in awe.

"Well, let's go try it on," Sigourney prodded.

"Yes, I want to try it on."

The three women walked into the boutique, and Sigourney approached the sales associate and pointed to the dress in the window. Soon Tess was swept away to the fitting room, while the sales associate collected her size from the storeroom.

The saleswoman helped Tess into the dress and carefully zipped up the back. "Let's step outside and show your friends."

Tess walked onto the boutique floor and stood on the platform in front of the three-way mirror.

Kate was beaming at her beautiful daughter.

Sigourney sighed. "Perfection."

"It's a little long, but the tailor can adjust the length for you," the associated informed Tess.

"I love it. This is the one, Mom. Don't you think?" Tess asked, all the worry over cost forgotten.

"It is."

"Okay, let me call alterations and we'll get this fitted for you. When do you need the dress ready?"

"Not until May. This is my wedding dress."

"Congratulations! You made a splendid choice."

"Thank you. Do you mind if I have a word with my mother before the tailor arrives?"

"Certainly, I'll go fetch some champagne."

The sales associate left the women as Kate and Sigourney approached the platform. Tess lifted her arm to show her mother the price tag. "Please don't faint, but this dress costs two thousand dollars."

"I told you I had some money saved. It's yours. You look so beautiful I'm going to cry," her mother said.

"No, please don't cry. You'll make me cry," Tess pleaded.

"I think that's a steal," Sigourney interrupted. "Just look at the craftsmanship. Lagerfeld's done wonders for the label since he took over the helm. It will be money well spent because you can wear it more than once."

"You still need a veil," her mother chimed in.

"No, I don't want a veil. It's perfect, just as it is."

"She's right, Kate. I think Sebastian's sense of style is rubbing off on Tess."

The sales associate came back with a silver tray containing three champagne flutes. Her co-worker was holding three boxes of shoes.

"You'll need to know what shoes you'll wear on your wedding day so we can get the length right. I have three different heel heights here. Try these on and tell me which one feels the most comfortable. Once we determine heel height, we can get your dress ready and go to the shoe department to find a pair you like."

It was a bit of a whirlwind—that morning she couldn't find anything she liked; that afternoon, she found the dress in fifteen minutes. She did feel a pang of regret for spending so much money on the dress, but Sigourney had a good point: Tess planned to wear the dress more than once. She had done it with the dresses Sebastian bought her at Bergdorf's, and this would be no different. She could even have it cut down to a tea-length to give her more options later on.

Tess was thrilled with the purchase. Maybe living with Sebastian was rubbing off on her, because she couldn't believe she'd just agreed to spend so much money on a dress.

An hour later, she thanked Sigourney for the company and escorted her mom to Penn Station. Then she headed back to the condo.

Tess walked through the front door of the condo holding a Saks shopping bag. She found Sebastian sitting on the sofa reading an art magazine. She put down the bag and walked over to her fiancé.

"How was your shopping trip?" he asked as he closed the magazine.

"I survived," she said, taking a seat next to him. "It actually wasn't that bad."

"So was it a successful trip?"

"I found a dress," Tess replied nonchalantly.

"Were you just settling to stop Sigourney from pulling you all over New York City in her quest for the perfect dress?"

Tess leaned in and kissed him on the lips. "I didn't settle. I found a dress I'm very happy with, and I'm not going to talk about it anymore. You're not to see the dress until I walk down the aisle."

"There is no aisle," he reminded her.

"Don't be difficult. You know what I mean," she pouted.

Sebastian took her in his arms and pulled her on top of him as he lay down on the couch. "I can't wait to see your dress—and more importantly, to be your husband."

Chapter 9 - Holiday

Sebastian entered Sigourney's brownstone and looked around. The place was quiet. "Sigourney," he bellowed from the bottom of the staircase, "Where the hell are you?"

"Don't get your knickers in a knot," she replied, jogging down the marble stairs.

"I only have an hour before I need to get back downtown to pick up Tess."

"Okay, it won't take that long."

They strolled into the sitting room and sat down. Sigourney poured tea from the service set out on the coffee table. She sat back and took a leisurely sip. Sebastian's patience was wearing thin.

"So why was I summoned?" he asked.

"What are the honeymoon plans?"

"I'm taking Tess to Europe for a few months. I told you that already."

"How are you going to pay for that?"

"We're getting a Euro-rail pass."

"You're slumming it?" she asked, disgusted by the idea.

"Sorry to disappoint you, but I'm not exactly in the position to shower Tess with five star accommodations and first class train tickets. Have you forgotten?" Sebastian let the tea cup go cold and walked over the sidebar to pour himself a finger of scotch.

"I'm handling this poorly," Sigourney admitted. "You both deserve a wonderful trip. You're starting your married life together. I want to give that to you as my wedding gift."

Sebastian placed the empty glass down the sideboard. "I can buy my wife a wedding trip," he rebuked, his ego wounded.

"Of course you can, darling, but Tess deserves grandeur and romance!"

"I'll have you know I'm very romantic. Honestly, if you just called me here to berate me, I have better things to do," he warned.

"Sebastian, you didn't see Tess' reaction when we went shopping for the wedding dress."

"I know her reaction. It was similar to having a root canal. She's not comfortable in that type of situation and I'm surprised she even agreed to go along with you."

"It started out that way, but when we left the bridal salon and started browsing the couture gowns, she became an entirely different girl," Sigourney told him, beaming with pride.

Sebastian took a seat on the chair across from his sister and cocked an eyebrow. "What are you talking about?"

"Tess didn't tell you anything about our shopping trip?" she queried.

"She said she had a nice day and she found a dress. I reckon she just picked something to stop you dragging her from one shop to the next."

Sigourney laughed aloud. "Tess was playing coy! She found the perfect dress and it's a Chanel."

Sebastian quietly studied his sister. Surely they weren't both talking about *his* Tess Hamilton. Tess all but begged him not to buy her a fancy dress on their first shopping trip. It didn't seem possible that conservative, thrifty Tess would spend money on a couture wedding gown.

"Did you buy her the dress?" he asked.

"No, I was fully prepared to—it was perfect for Tess. Her mother had saved some money for the wedding reception, and she said Tess should use it to buy the dress, since you're having the ceremony at home."

Sebastian shook his head in disbelief. "She used the money to buy a dress?"

"Your appreciation for designer clothes is rubbing off on your fiancée." Sigourney grinned. "And that is why I want to give you both a honeymoon trip. Even if it's just the first week—let me lavish you in luxury."

"So what exactly did you have in mind?" Sebastian asked with curiosity, leaning back in the chair and crossing his legs.

"Two tickets on the Concord and a week at the George V."

Sebastian's mouth dropped open at the suggestion. It was a truly generous offer, worth thousands of dollars—and something he would love to do for Tess, but couldn't afford to do. He wanted to respond, but she had left him speechless.

"Cat got your tongue?"

"It's too much, Sigourney. You've stunned even me."

Sigourney stood from the sofa and walked over to her brother and sat on the arm of his chair. "It's not enough after what Mummy did to you," she said in all seriousness. "Anywho, I get a portion of your inheritance, so just think of it as me spending your money on you."

Sebastian laughed aloud. "When you put it that way, I have no reservations whatsoever in accepting your gift." He thought for a moment than added, "Please feel free to throw in the first class Euro-rail passes while you are at it."

Sigourney swatted his arm, then leaned in and kissed him on the cheek. "I'm so very happy for the two of you. I'm glad you accepted my gift."

"Can you keep it a secret? I want to surprise Tess."

"She'll need a trousseau. How will she know what to buy?" his sister inquired.

"Whoa, slow down. How are you going to keep it a secret if you drag her on another shopping spree?"

"Sebastian, she can't fly on the Concord and eat at the George V in jeans and a sweatshirt," Sigourney admonished.

"Yes, I know. We need a plan, though. Let me think about it. Maybe if we get Kate involved," Sebastian reasoned.

"Okay, thinking caps on."

Sebastian glanced down at his Rolex. "I have to get going." He stood and hugged Sigourney. "You are brilliant, darling sister. Thank you."

"You're welcome. Let's have lunch next week at Sardi's and we'll plan some more. Ring me with your schedule."

"I'll do that," Sebastian agreed.

Sebastian made his way back downtown and found Tess in the NYU library, books piled high on the table in front of her. He was so excited about Sigourney's gift that he could hardly contain his delight, grinning like a fool.

"What are you so happy about?" Tess asked, looking up from her book.

"Everything," he replied with enthusiasm.

"I know that look," Tess warned. "You're up to something."

"I'm sworn to secrecy."

"Then that must mean Sigourney's involved."

Sebastian steered the conversation in a different direction, lest he get too exhilarated and reveal his sister's grand plan. "How much longer will you need? When can we go home?"

Tess studied her notes and then looked at the books stacked in front of her. "I probably need an hour."

"Okay," he agreed without argument. Sebastian reached into this backpack and pulled out a notebook. If Tess had to study, then he would make notes regarding their honeymoon. Sigourney was right: Tess would need a trousseau. He knew her sizes, so all he had to do was list the items she would need. Making the list of lingerie and outfits while letting his imagination contemplate Tess in various stages of being undressed was the most enjoyable time Sebastian had ever spent in a library.

* * *

Tess was grateful for Sebastian's silence. Actually, she was stunned. Sebastian was acting out of character and she wondered if Sigourney had spilled the details to him about her wedding dress. He was scribbling away in his notebook with the most blissful look on his face: his sapphire colored eyes dancing with delight, his square jaw relaxed, lips upturned. What was he thinking about? As much as she enjoyed watching him, she had to get back to work. The paper due by the end of the week wasn't going to write itself, so Tess reluctantly averted her gaze and continued her work.

When they stepped out of the library, snow had begun to fall. The iridescent flakes covering Washington Square made it look like a picture-perfect post card. The snow was always pretty when it first fell. It wasn't until later, after salt, cinders, and footprints made it dirty and slushy, that the beauty lost its appeal.

"I'm hungry. Can we grab dinner before we catch the ferry back?" Tess asked.

"Let me guess—McDonald's?"

She gave him a big toothy grin. He really must have had a great day if he so readily agreed to the fast food joint.

"You're in luck. There's one on the next corner. Imagine that!" Sebastian ribbed with jest.

Tess wrapped her arm around his waist and leaned into him. "Thank you."

"Anything for you, darling," he replied as they reached their destination and he held open the door.

They sat at a table in front of the window, watching New Yorkers pass by while they ate their cheeseburgers.

"I was thinking we need to buy you some luggage for Europe," Sebastian said as he sipped his coffee.

"How much luggage could I possibly need? If we're going from city to city, I don't want to drag around a lot of bags. Don't you have something I can use?"

"You'll need a few nice outfits for when we go out to dinner. I love you, but I'm not traipsing through Europe and only eating at McDonald's," he replied, taking her hand in his.

Tess' eyes lit with excitement. "I love that idea. I could write a travel log of the McDonald's throughout Europe—talk about the different items on the menu that pertain to the locale."

"Give out Michelin stars," he playfully interrupted. "Yes, I'm sure it will be a best seller," Sebastian replied, deadpan.

Tess loved provoking him, especially about fast food restaurants. It felt so good to be with him like this—carefree and lighthearted. Finally, they were falling back into their old habits. It was a relief and Tess was so thankful that they were able to get over her indiscretion with Dan Miller. She would honestly give Sebastian anything he desired because she wanted to prove to him that she was committed to their relationship.

"Where would you like to go to buy me luggage?" she asked.

"Macy's?"

Tess was pleased with his response: maybe her thriftiness was wearing off on Sebastian. No—who was she trying to kid? Sebastian would never be thrifty. He was most likely just learning to pick and choose his battles. Tess did need the luggage, so it seemed like a good idea.

"Okay, Macy's it is. Do you want to stop and look before we head back home?"

"Perfect," Sebastian agreed.

Chapter 10 - Art for Art's Sake

Sebastian was watching the early morning news while Tess was in the bathroom getting ready for class. Breaking news came across the bottom of the screen, and he read it with great interest.

When Tess joined him in the living room, he was staring at the painting above the fireplace, lost in thought.

"Hey, are you okay?" Tess asked gingerly, stepping up behind him.

"Andy Warhol just died this morning in New York Hospital," he whispered in disbelief.

"Why was he in the hospital?"

"Gallbladder surgery."

"You shouldn't die from routine surgery."

"No, you shouldn't," he agreed. "That painting just increased its value tenfold," Sebastian said in a subdued voice, pointing to the oxidation painting.

Tess chuckled until she realized he wasn't joking. "Seriously? That much?"

"I never joke about art. I told you it would pay for our children's college education one day. I just didn't think it would be so soon."

"I'm sorry this makes you so sad," Tess said.

"The world lost a great artist today." He looked down at his watch. They had to be leaving if they wanted to catch the ferry. "We need to get going."

They rode on the ferry in silence, and then switched over to the subway to get to NYU. "I've got to meet with Sigourney today after class, and then I have work at the gallery. Are you okay to make it home on your own? I don't know how late I'll be." Sebastian always escorted Tess, but today he was out of sorts.

"I can take care of myself, Sebastian. I don't need a bodyguard," Tess reassured him. "Go do what you need to do."

"Thank you. Ring me at the gallery when you arrive home safe, so I don't worry."

Tess kissed him goodbye. "I will."

After his class, Sebastian met Sigourney at Bloomingdale's for lunch. They were meeting to discuss a bridal shower for Tess. Even though their ceremony wouldn't be traditional, Sebastian wanted Tess to experience everything a normal bride got to experience.

Sigourney had her planner and pen at the ready, while Sebastian perused the notes he had jotted down in his notebook. "I think we should have it at the brownstone. You can tell Tess I've invited you both to dinner."

"That will work. I need to check with Kate to make sure she can get off work."

"I'll take care of the invites, just give me the info. I know this is a small affair, but is there anyone else you want to invite? Any old school chums that Tess might have?"

Sebastian pondered the idea. Tess hadn't kept in touch with Jordan or Courtney. All of her time had been devoted to NYU and Sebastian. He had to admit he liked it that way, even if he had to vie for attention with her class work. "She has an Aunt that lives in Florida. You can ask Kate about that. I've never met her."

The waiter brought the siblings' soup and salad and placed it on the table. Sebastian picked up his spoon and took a sip of the asparagus soup. "Oh, and add Penny Stanton to the list. If she can fly in, I know Tess would like that."

"Tess knows Penny?" Sigourney inquired, then took a bite of her salad.

"Yes, they met last year when Penny visited Edgewood."

"Wonderful, consider it done! It will be so nice to see her again." They continued eating lunch while each one of them individually made additional notes in their books. "What about the trousseau?"

"I have a list. I thought we could purchase what Tess needs after lunch."

"Let me see your list."

They passed each other their respective notes. It was the odd brother/sister dynamic they shared. Sebastian appreciated that Sigourney was on the same wavelength: it kept her quiet. God knows she was chatty, and he really enjoyed when they could spend time together without talking.

When they had finished their meal, Sigourney placed thirty dollars on the table and they made their way to the women's clothing floor and spent the next hour shopping for all the items on Sebastian's list. He had Bloomingdale's deliver the items to Sigourney's address, since they were bridal shower gifts for Tess. He knew it was unusual for the groom to buy his bride a shower gift, but Tess didn't have many friends or extended family, so he was determined to do this for her.

Fiona was on the phone when Sebastian stepped foot in the gallery. She gave a little wave as he made his way to the back room to hang up his coat and scarf.

"How are things today?" Sebastian inquired, stepping onto the sales floor.

"Crazy—I've been fielding calls from clients looking to get their hands on a Warhol."

"It was sad news."

"Yes, and the sharks are circling and they haven't even buried the poor man yet," Fiona agreed.

"They're just looking for a good investment. I know this is a business, but if I were you, I'd sell to the collector that loved his work, not the person looking to make a quick buck."

Fiona gave Sebastian a long, hard look, her lips curving up into a smile. "That's exactly what I'm going to do. You're a brilliant protégé."

"I have an excellent teacher."

"Always the charmer—don't ever change. Business is up since you joined me."

"So who's on the short list for the silkscreen?" Sebastian asked, walking over the desk.

Fiona pointed to a list of three names: the first was Evan Bloomfield, the second was Abigail Archibald, and the third was Alexander Kilmoore.

"I like Mrs. Archibald. She's always so pleasant when she comes in."

"That's because she treats you as if you were her favorite grandchild!"

"There's nothing wrong with that!"

"Especially when you sell her paintings and make me a profit."

"Bloomfield is too full of himself. He may be a true art lover, but he'll be a pompous arse if you sell it to him."

"True," Fiona conceded. "What about Kilmoore?"

"I like Kilmoore, but pop art really isn't his thing. Give it to Mrs. Archibald. It will look great next to her Liechtenstein."

"A wise choice. You keep this up, Irons, and you could be running this gallery in ten years."

"Oh, I hope it won't take that long," Sebastian joked.

Fiona patted him on the back. "I have a phone call to make. Mind the shop."

"Yes, ma'am."

Sebastian made his way home around eight o'clock. Tess was up in the loft, seated at the desk, studying. He climbed the steps and greeted her with a kiss. "How was your day?"

"Good. How was yours?"

"Very busy, but I got a lot accomplished," Sebastian said. "The gallery was swarming with phone calls."

"Everybody wants a Warhol, huh?"

"Yes, and Fiona only had one to sell."

"So did it go to the highest bidder?" Tess asked.

"No," Sebastian said with pride. "Fiona sold it to the person who would appreciate it the most."

"Well, then all is right in the world." Tess smiled as she closed her book and stood from the desk, giving him a hug. "Should I even ask what you and Sigourney are up to?"

"Secret plans, can't say."

Tess shook her head. "When the two of you get together, I need to watch out. Something extravagant is bound to happen."

"Oh please, you love my surprises!" he playfully exclaimed.

"Correction—I love you. I tolerate the surprises because you get so excited planning them."

"Not true —you loved the birthday dinner here at home."

"Okay, let me rephrase: I love when the surprises are inexpensive and homemade. But then you did pull out a Cartier diamond at the end, so technically, it really wasn't an inexpensive surprise."

Sebastian took her hand in his and examined the diamond ring. "I watch you sometimes. You look down at that ring and move it around so it catches the light and sparkles. Then those gorgeous lips curl up into a smile and I know you could never be angry with me for buying it."

"You're right," she blushed. "Come downstairs, I'll make you a sandwich. You must be hungry."

Chapter 11 - You're The Best Thing That Ever Happened To Me

Sebastian placed a Diet Coke in front of Tess. She'd been sitting at the table for the past three hours, studying for her finals. She needed a break and he didn't know how to get her out of the cocoon she had created around herself. He cracked the tab on the soda can and the familiar sound of fizzing bubbles caught her attention.

"Take a break."

"Too much to do," she said, briefly looking up at him.

"You work too hard."

"Aren't you worried about your finals?"

"No, I have more important things to think about."

That comment certainly gained her attention. Tess closed the book and studied him with intensity. "What could possibly be more important?"

Sebastian held his mouth shut, attempting not to laugh, but his smiling eyes gave him away. "Gee, I don't know. Our wedding is only a week away."

"You said you would take care of everything, and all I had to do was show up," she remarked, slightly annoyed at his interruption.

"I have taken care of everything but Sigourney rang and asked if we could come for lunch on Saturday. What shall I tell her?"

Tess opened the text book on the table and refocused her attention on it. "Fine, we can go, but please tell me we're not going to the Russian Tea Room."

"No, it's just a luncheon at the brownstone."

"Good, I can pick up my wedding dress at that time."

That was the most they had conversed over the past few days, and Sebastian felt lucky to get that much time from her. He leaned over and kissed the top of her head. "I'm going to bed. Don't stay up too late."

"Love you," she absentmindedly replied as she continued to read.

Sebastian backed away, watching Tess as she sipped her Coke and read in deep concentration. He turned off the main light and quietly closed the bedroom door. In a week's time she would be his bride, and he couldn't wait.

* * *

With her last exam finally over, Tess felt she could breathe a little easier—just a little. Sebastian had been so wonderful to her over the past week: leaving her alone to study, not pestering her about the wedding. She'd been so focused on school, the wedding fell to the back of her mind. She was happy to be marrying him, she just didn't get excited over all the pomp and circumstance like he did. That was something that definitely made their relationship different.

She was glad to get out of the condo and have lunch with Sigourney, even though the conversation would surely turn to wedding talk. That was okay—she could just sit back and enjoy her meal while Sebastian and Sigourney debated which chairs to rent or what type of flowers should be purchased. Tess was so grateful it hadn't become the overblown affair Sebastian had initially wanted. She just let him run the plans within the confines of a small, intimate ceremony.

Sebastian opened the door to the brownstone and let Tess enter first. The sitting room doors were closed, which was unusual because Sigourney spent so much time in that room playing the piano.

"Sigourney, we're here," he yelled up the stairs. Sigourney didn't respond. "Maybe she's in here," Sebastian said, opening the double doors to the sitting room.

"Surprise!"

Tess stopped breathing for a moment when she looked inside the room. Her mom, Sigourney, Alice, and Penny were standing to welcome her. She looked at Sebastian, "What's all this?"

"Your bridal shower. You don't think Sigourney would let you get away without one."

"I've been too busy to even think about it," Tess admitted.

"That's why it was so easy to plan!" Sigourney explained, coming forward to hug Tess.

Tess greeted everyone and took a seat in the place of honor. There were gifts piled high on the coffee table—far more gifts than people in attendance. The siblings were being extravagant after all, and there was nothing Tess could do about it, so she let them have their fun.

"Penny, it's so good to see you. How long are you in town?" Tess asked.

"I flew in for the wedding. Sebastian is the first of our group to tie the knot. I couldn't miss it."

"I'm glad you're here. I can't wait to see what other surprises my fiancé has planned for me," she said, grinning at Sebastian, who sat on the arm of her chair.

"Are you pleased?" he leaned down and whispered in her ear.

"Yes, this was a lovely surprise."

"Okay, you two love birds. Time for gifts!" Sigourney handed Tess a small long box.

Inside Tess found an ivory lace garter trimmed with blue satin ribbon, and a note from her mom.

I wore this on my wedding day to your father. I wish you and Sebastian all the happiness and love in the world. Love, Mom

Tess stood up and hugged her mom. "This means so much to me. I love you."

Next, Sigourney handed Tess an envelope. She opened the card to find another handwritten note.

Sebastian told me how much you loved London. Please accept this gift and enjoy a week's stay at the Savoy during your honeymoon trip, since I know how

*much you both love the accommodations. Best wishes,
Penny*

"That's brilliant, Pen. Thank you," Sebastian said,
kissing her on the cheek.

Tess was happy. She was fully prepared to
backpack across Europe, so this was an unexpected
and welcome surprise. "Penny, it's too much, but we
really will enjoy this. I can't thank you enough."

* * *

Sebastian heard the front door of the brownstone
open. He wondered who else Sigourney may have
invited, because he wasn't expecting anyone else.
Who would just let themselves in unannounced? He
turned to look in the direction of the front door as
Tess continued opening her gifts.

There, standing in the open doorway, was Lady
Irons. Sebastian felt his heart drop to the bottom of
his stomach. He frantically looked at Sigourney. This
couldn't be happening.

"Excuse me, please," Sigourney announced to the
her guests as she stood and quickly headed for her
mother, pushing her back into the hall and closing
the double doors behind them.

"What's going on?" Tess asked, the look on her
face intense and confused.

Sebastian shook his head. "I don't know. This wasn't planned." He tapped his foot on the floor in irritation. "I have to go. Sigourney can't take the blame for this." He stood and bolted toward the doors.

"Sigourney, what is going on?" Lady Irons demanded.

"Mummy, what are you doing here?"

"I had a layover coming back from Japan. I thought I'd come visit for a few hours."

"You could have warned me," Sigourney reasoned in exasperation.

Sebastian stepped into the vestibule. "Are you okay, Sigourney?"

"Of course. Why wouldn't I be?"

"I think you need to leave. You weren't invited to the party," Sebastian said to Lily in a sinister voice.

Lady Irons ignored Sebastian and looked at Sigourney instead. "I specifically told you that I didn't want you to have any contact with him. Have you forgotten?"

"Mummy, Sebastian is my brother. I'm not going to stop speaking to him just because you two had a falling out."

"Oh, is that what we're calling it?" Sebastian snickered.

Sigourney grabbed Sebastian by the suit coat and pulled him away, saying under her breath, "You're not helping me. Go back inside and tend to the guests. I'm fine."

Sebastian opened his mouth to protest, but Sigourney gave him a dirty look that effectively shut him up. He nodded his head in agreement and joined the ladies in the sitting room.

The double doors opened and Sebastian appeared. Tess walked over to him. "What's happening?"

"Sigourney has it under control." He turned to the other ladies. "Why don't I refresh your drinks?" He walked around the room and filled their champagne glasses.

Alice reached out and patted his hand in support. "That was unexpected."

"Yes."

"Let's pass around the canapés until Sigourney comes back," Alice suggested.

They both went to the kitchen and came back a short time later, offering food to Tess, Kate, and Penny. The five of them sat quietly nibbling away until Sigourney joined them.

She breezed into the room with a smile on her face, as if nothing had occurred. "I'm sorry for the interruption. Tess, please continue to open your gifts."

"I'm sorry if I put you in a difficult situation," Tess apologized. "Please tell me she didn't disown you, too."

With a wave of her hand, she dismissed her worry. "I'm the favorite, she won't disown me."

Sebastian studied Sigourney. She may have looked cool, calm, and collected, but Lily's visit had rattled her. Everyone was looking at his sister. "She's right. Sigourney has always been the favorite. If Lily keeps kicking everyone out of the family, she'll have no one to inherit all her money," he said to make light of the situation.

Sigourney was the only person to find the humor in his statement and laughed aloud. "Enough drama for today. We have more presents to open."

* * *

Tess continued making her way through the pile of presents that sat before her. When she finally finished opening the gifts, she had a new wardrobe for her honeymoon, a beautifully hand-stitched quilt from Alice, and a crystal and pearl beaded headband to wear with her wedding dress.

It was an overwhelming day. Talk about one extreme to the other! It wore Tess out and she was suddenly tired.

"Sigourney, thank you for the bridal shower. I do hope everything is okay between you and your mother."

"No worries, Tess. I can handle her."

Sebastian came up behind the two and placed his hand on the small of Tess' back. "I've hired a car to take us home. Your mother and Alice can ride along. Are you ready to go?"

They dropped Tess' mom off at Penn Station to catch the train back to Philadelphia. Alice went back to her condo, leaving Sebastian and Tess alone with a pile of presents neatly stacked in the center of the living room.

"What a day," Tess said as she cuddled with Sebastian. "Are you sure you're okay?"

"It was a little bumpy there for a moment," he admitted, "but I'm fine. Did you like your gifts?"

"It was too much, Sebastian. I'll be the best dressed backpacker in Europe."

"You need a few nice outfits if we're staying at the Savoy."

"And God knows where else you've booked," she chided.

"That part is a surprise."

"I'm so looking forward to it. You were right. I'm exhausted. I need some downtime, and I'm happy to spend the next three months alone with you."

Chapter 12 - Your Big Day

Alice and Henry hosted a wedding breakfast in their condo, with Sebastian, Tess, and Kate Hamilton in attendance. The group sat around the table, relaxed and happy.

"I can't believe how calm you look, Tess. I was a bundle of nerves on my wedding day!" Alice exclaimed as she cleared the breakfast plates.

"And you're bucking tradition by seeing the groom before the ceremony," Henry added.

"Very few things about this wedding have been traditional. Why should I start now?" Tess responded, reaching over to take Sebastian's hand.

"Then let me come downstairs and get ready with you," Sebastian suggested.

"No—out of the question. I want the dress reveal to be a surprise. You're always surprising me. Now it's my turn."

"Okay, Tess. We should be going downstairs to get you ready," her mom said, pushing back from the table.

Sebastian walked his fiancée to the front door. "I'll see you in ninety minutes," he whispered, kissing her on the lips.

Sigourney was fluttering about as Tess and Kate entered the condo. "Everything under control?" Tess asked as Sigourney moved about like a drill sergeant.

"Almost ready to go. Go have a shower. The hairdresser will be here in fifteen minutes."

Tess saluted her soon to be sister-in-law and headed for the bathroom.

Sitting at the vanity, Tess watched as the hairdresser placed the beaded headband on her head. She slowly stood up from the vanity and turned to face her mom, who tried to hold back a tear.

"Don't cry, Mom. You'll make me cry and then I'll ruin my makeup."

"I have never seen you more beautiful. I love you, honey."

Tess hugged her mother. "I love you, too."

"Let's get you out of the robe and into your wedding dress."

Tess carefully slipped into the Chanel gown and turned around so her mom could zip it up. Tess smoothed out the tulle skirt and smiled. She couldn't wait for Sebastian so see her in her new dress.

Next she slipped on the blue satin garter— something old and blue. The headband was something new. "I don't have anything borrowed," she fretted.

There was a knock on the door. Sigourney popped her head inside the room. "You look absolutely amazing, Tess." She walked into the room, holding something in her hand. "I would be honored if you'd wear this today. It was Sebastian and my grandmother's diamond bracelet."

Tess looked at the ornate yet delicate nineteenth century piece. "I don't know what to say. It's so beautiful."

"Being a countess has its advantages, and Granpapa did love to shower her with jewels," Sigourney explained. "Put out your wrist."

Tess let Sigourney secure the bracelet. "Something borrowed," she said to her mother.

"We're all set. Kate, do you want to take your seat?" Sigourney asked.

They left the room, leaving Tess alone. She thought she should be nervous, but it was the complete opposite. She was comfortable and at ease. Even though she had fought Sebastian on the date, she knew in her heart the time was right. Marrying him was right and she couldn't wait to become Mrs. Sebastian Irons.

Sade's *Cherish the Day* began to play. This was her cue. She picked up the small bouquet of white and pink roses and opened the bedroom door. Across the room, in front of the full-length window with the view of Manhattan, stood Sebastian. He was wearing a tuxedo, his brown hair perfectly groomed and his sapphire blue eyes sparkling with excitement. He was the most gorgeous man she had ever laid eyes on. She smiled back at him and started her walk across the room to join him.

* * *

Tess was stunning. Sebastian reminded himself to keep his mouth shut, lest he look like a fool agape at her beauty. The dress was perfect. The sheer tulle skirt, in the palest pink he had ever seen, suited her perfectly. The fitted bodice and beaded short sleeves showed off her creamy skin. Her brown hair was pulled up, showing off her slender neck. Even he could never have picked such a spectacular gown. She couldn't get to him fast enough and Sebastian wanted to rush to her and kiss her for all he was worth.

When she joined him, Sebastian took her hand and, leaning into her, he whispered. "You take my breath away."

Tess blushed at his comment and together they turned to face the justice of the peace. He greeted the guests and began the ceremony.

Tess handed her bouquet to Sigourney before Sebastian took her hands and recited his vows. Gazing into her eyes, he began: "I thought I might quote a poem to express my feelings for you, but no matter how beautiful the words, they just seem to pale in comparison and they could never express how deeply I love you. You are the most beautiful person I have ever known. I am in awe of your grace, caring, tenacity, and ambition. I'm not sure how I lived before you came into my life, but I am certain that I could never face another day without you by my side. I never thought that being someone's soul mate was possible—but you make me believe the impossible. I used to tell Nanny that I loved her more than anything in the world, but you—you are my world, Tess. I love you with everything I am and everything I hope to be. I promise to spend every day for the rest of my life loving and cherishing you."

The timbre in his voice, the feeling in his eyes, and the way he poured his emotions into the vows simply melted her heart. A few delicate tears ran down her cheeks. When it was her turn to speak, she decided to forgo the speech she had written ahead of time. After hearing how Sebastian felt, her speech seemed inadequate and rehearsed. She decided to forget the written text and spoke these words from her heart.

"You are the most amazing man I know: my best friend, my partner, my everything. I can't even properly describe what I feel for you—the depth of the love I have for you. It would take a lifetime to do that, and that's what I intend to do. I will show you every day how in love I am with you, Sebastian."

Sebastian slipped the gold band on her ring finger while pledging his troth. Tess followed and slipped the wedding ring on his ring finger.

"I hereby pronounce you husband and wife. You can kiss your bride," the justice of the peace concluded.

Everyone in the room clapped, but Sebastian didn't hear any of it. He simply honed in on his wife's supple lips and kissed her with abandon. When they finally pulled apart, they were surrounded by their family and good wishes.

* * *

They danced to *No Ordinary Love* in the middle of the living room and Tess felt complete contentment. "I'm so happy right now," she told Sebastian as she nuzzled against his shoulder.

"You were right the entire time—having the wedding here was perfect."

They posed for photos, mingled with their guests, until it was time to cut the cake. Sigourney had outdone herself by having the cake made by the go-to cake maker in Manhattan. It was a two-tiered round cake, draped in white fondant and covered with fresh flowers. It was almost too pretty to cut. After removing the top layer, Tess and Sebastian joined hands over the sterling silver cake knife and then cut a slice. They shared the first piece, carefully feeding each other, to avoid spilling anything on their clothing. The chocolate cake with raspberry filling melted in Tess' mouth. "I could eat this whole cake," she whispered to Sebastian, who was beaming down at her.

"Later, in bed," he whispered before kissing her.

When the reception was over, Sebastian closed and locked the door. Leaning against the door, he admired his new wife, whose back was turned to him as she looked across the Hudson as the sun set over the city.

When he finally came up behind her and wrapped his arms around her waist, she let out a languid sigh. "Perfect ending to a perfect day."

"Perfect life," Sebastian corrected, kissing her neck. "You look so amazing in this dress, but I can't wait to get you out of it."

Tess giggled. "Be careful. It cost a fortune and I need to pack it for Europe."

Sebastian carefully unzipped the gown and slowly slipped if off her shoulders. With great care, he draped the dress over the back of the chair. He got down on one knee and admired her beauty as she stood in front of him wearing lacy white lingerie.

He took her hand and pulled her down so she sat on his knee. "I know we have an early flight tomorrow, but I need to spend the night making love to you."

The corner of her mouth turned up as she nodded her head in agreement. "Sleep is overrated, anyway."

"Indeed." Sebastian picked her up and carried her to their bedroom.

* * *

"Are you happy, Mrs. Irons?" Sebastian asked, holding his wife in his arms after they made love.

"Very happy, Mr. Irons," she replied, looking up at him. "Do I get to learn a little bit more about our honeymoon now? You and Sigourney have had your heads together for months planning this and I can't help but think it will be grandiose."

"Henry will be here at seven o'clock tomorrow morning to take us to JFK. From there we're taking the Concorde to Paris."

"The Concorde! We can't afford that!"

"The honeymoon trip is Sigourney's gift to us, or as she puts it, she's simply spending the cut of my inheritance she gets."

"She's done too much. How can we repay her?" Tess questioned with worry.

"Shh," he muttered, placing his lips over hers. "We're only doing this once, remember? I want you to enjoy it."

His kisses made her feel dreamy, like she was floating on a cloud. "When do we get to go to London?"

"We will start with a week in Paris at the George V and head to the Cote D'Azur, cross over into Spain and visit Barcelona and Madrid."

"What about Vienna? I want pastries!" she exclaimed.

"I'll buy you pastries in every city we visit." Sebastian promised. "We'll end up in London and catch the plane back home from Heathrow."

She was so excited that she all but jumped up and down on the bed. "Am I going to have enough clothes?"

"Sigourney has packed for you. We'll have the concierge launder the clothes when we run out."

Tess looked down at her rings and then looked into Sebastian's eyes. "Thank you—for everything. I can't wait to leave."

Chapter 13 - No Ordinary Love

The Concorde landed at Charles de Gaulle airport three and a half hours after they departed JFK. They took a taxi into Paris, their destination the George V hotel on Avenue George V, just off the Champs Elysees.

Their room was adorned with white and gold accented Louis XIV furniture. The bed was a four-poster canopy with ostrich plumes jutting from the top of the posts, replete with light blue and gold embroidered silk linens, and rose petals scattered on top the duvet. Tess eagerly walked around the room and looked in the armoire, checked out the marble bathroom, and finally stopped in front of the window that overlooked the Eiffel Tower.

"It's so—" she stopped, lost for words.

"French," Sebastian finished, coming up behind her and placing his hands on her waist. He turned her around to face him and untied the knot of her belt of the Diane von Furstenberg wrap dress she was wearing while he continued. "Ornate, elaborate, ostentatious."

"Yes, all of those things." She slipped out of her wrap dress, saying, "You know how turned on I get when you use fancy words."

"And speak in a British accent," he cooed, sitting in a nearby chair and pulling her onto his lap.

"Make love to me, Mr. Irons."

"It would be my pleasure, Mrs. Irons."

Sebastian picked up Tess and playfully threw her onto the bed; rose petals bounced into the air as she landed on the soft mattress. He stripped out of his clothes and crawled toward her, planting little kisses along her body. Then he took one of the stray rose petals and ran it along her cleavage and over her pebbled nipples.

Tess grabbed the linens in her fist. "Too slow," she whispered.

"Not slow enough," Sebastian countered. "I plan to make love to you at a leisurely pace, working you into a frenzy until you are delirious with pleasure."

"I don't think I can wait that long, Sebastian."

"Patience, Tess." He reached over and grabbed his silk tie. "Put your hands together."

Tess followed his order and soon he was wrapping the tie around her wrists and lifting her arms over her head.

* * *

Tess was taken aback at the move. She wasn't afraid of sex, but yet again, Sebastian had surprised her. They had never done anything like this in the bedroom, and Tess couldn't help but feel a pang of excitement as she relinquished control.

Sebastian leaned back on his knees and stared at Tess, lying there in her bra, panties, and garter belt. He watched her chest rapidly rise and fall in anticipation of his next move. He slipped off her panties and spread her legs, the cool air touching her and making her shiver. Sliding his hands up and down her inner thighs, he leaned in and kissed her belly. Sebastian's tongue trailed down her middle to her clit.

She let out an audible gasp as she felt his tongue flick back and forth. He was teasing her, long and slow, like he promised. Tess had other ideas. She took her tied wrists, which were above her head, and reached down to grab his hair. Sebastian looked up at her face, a mischievous look in his eye, and then his tongue resumed its languid pace.

Next she felt two fingers inside her, stroking her. That movement in connection with his tongue set her nerves on fire. Tess bucked her hips up to spur him on. She needed him to go faster—so close to coming. He must have sensed it, for he suddenly stopped.

"No!" Tess cried out at the loss of his touch. "Don't leave me."

Sebastian gave her a wicked grin. "I'm not through with you yet." He pushed her arms back above her head and gently rolled Tess over onto her stomach. Then he began to massage her shoulders and back. It felt wonderful, but it wasn't what Tess wanted. She whimpered under his touch.

"Don't you like this?"

"No, I need to feel you inside me. Stop torturing me, Sebastian."

"Is this torture? It feels like heaven to me," he said, lying down on top of her, his erection nestled against her ass. Sebastian reached around and cupped her breasts.

Tess wiggled her ass to see if she could wear down his resolve. He merely knelt behind her and playfully spanked her bare ass cheek. She was losing patience and her own sanity. If she could only untie the knot and free her hands, she would have pleasured herself. "Damn it, Bas, if you don't fuck me right now, you'll get no sex for the rest of this honeymoon," she ground out with need.

Sebastian chuckled. "Bas—you know I don't like nicknames. But I do like your conviction and sense of urgency. Lean back on your knees and I'll give you what you want, Tess."

She complied with his request, and with one smooth move, Sebastian was inside her. It wasn't slow and methodical, this time. No, this time he was thrusting with such intensity the bed shook as if it would break and they'd end up in a pile of satin and silk and splintered wood on the floor.

The sound of bare skin slapping together filled the room and as his cock hit her in just the right spot, she screamed into the pillow. The force of the orgasm was unlike anything she had ever experienced before.

With a few more quick thrusts, Sebastian came inside her. Her knees collapsed onto the bed as she felt the strong spasm of his twitching cock. Sebastian turned Tess on her side and held her close. "You are incredible," he managed to say between labored breaths. He reached out and began to untie the knot that confined her wrists.

"I think we ruined your tie," Tess commented as the piece of silk fell away and her hands were freed.

"I have plenty of ties," he muttered as he kissed her shoulder, which was glistening with perspiration. "Let's have a nice long bath."

* * *

Sebastian drew a bath while Tess lay in bed with a dreamy expression of satisfaction on her face. What had just transpired between them was the hottest sex he had ever had. The summer was poised to be the best of his life—their lives.

"The water is perfect, come join me," he called from the bathroom.

Tess walked into the room and stepped into the tub, sitting between Sebastian's legs. It was a claw foot monstrosity that could easily accommodate three people. Sebastian began to wash Tess' back with a sea sponge, the luxurious lather cleansing her skin.

"Why did you call me Bas?" he asked as he poured water over her back to rinse the away the soap.

"I don't know," she admitted, leaning back against his chest. "In the heat of the moment it just came out."

"You never talked dirty to me before. I liked it."

"You're one to be cheeky!"

"Cheeky Bas, I think I like it."

"If we're going to have sex like this all summer, we'll be too tired to do any sightseeing."

"That's not a bad thing in my book," Sebastian remarked.

"I'm not spending my entire European summer indoors. If all you wanted to do was make love, we could have stayed at home and saved the money."

"All right, then I'll show you the wonders of Europe by day and spend the evenings showing you the wonders of 'cheeky Bas.'"

Tess laughed aloud. "I'm starving. Can we order room service?"

"Anything for you, darling."

* * *

After feasting on fluffy omelets and fresh fruit, they drifted off to sleep, their stomachs full and their desire sated. They slept through the night to ten o'clock the next morning, the sun peeking through the curtains.

Tess stirred in Sebastian's arms. "Good morning," he whispered.

"Hmm," was all she could manage.

"Ready to start exploring the City of Lights?"

"Yes," she replied, opening her eyes. "What do you have in store for us today?"

"Breakfast and then Notre Dame on the Île de la Cité. There's a fantastic crepe shop nearby I know you'll love."

"You're making my mouth water just talking about it. Let's get dressed!" She sprang from the bed and rushed into the bathroom.

Tess dressed in a black skirt and cotton short-sleeved blouse, opting for her well-worn ballet flats, since they would be doing a lot of walking. Sebastian dressed in black trousers and gray button-down shirt, rolling up the sleeves to his elbows.

They walked along the cobbled streets of Paris, Tess in awe of its quaint cafés, vast open gardens, and many bridges. "Is it true what they say—that Paris is for lovers?"

Sebastian wrapped his arm around her shoulder. "I think it is. This is the first time I've ever been to Paris with someone I loved."

His remark made her smile. "I'll always remember this—the warm sun on our faces, the cool breeze in the air, how very much I love you."

Sebastian came to a stop on the Ponte Neuf bridge and pulled Tess into his arms. Ignoring the tourists, he kissed her with such passion that it took her breath away.

They toured the Norte Dame Cathedral. Tess admired the gothic architecture: the spire, the stained glass windows, and the great organ. Being Catholic, Tess had attended many church services and had been in many churches. This was so large and magnificent, she felt nothing but awe and reverence inside the massive place of worship.

When they exited the cathedral, Sebastian walked Tess across the street to the small shop and ordered two chocolate crepes. He handed one to Tess and then gave the cashier a few francs. They walked out of the shop and sat on a bench.

Tess took a bite of the crepe. It tasted like hazelnut. "I thought it was chocolate."

"French chocolate is mixed with hazelnut. This is the French's equivalent of fast food. Do you like it?"

She nodded her head. "Yeah, I do. It just wasn't what I expected."

"Wait till I take you to Laudrée."

"I don't know what that is, but I can't wait." Tess finished her crepe and sighed with happiness. "Where to next?"

"Musee D'Orsay—we'll take the metro."

After wandering around the art museum and eating dinner in a romantic café, Sebastian stopped by

Laudrée and purchased a box of macarons. Tess marveled at the pale green interior and colorful pastel confections with flavors like rose, pistachio, violet, and chocolate coconut.

Back at the hotel, Tess was lounging in a bubble bath, relaxing after their long day. Sebastian entered the bathroom with Tess' Nikon in hand.

"What are you doing with my camera?" she asked in a leery tone of voice.

"Taking pictures," he replied as he looked through the viewfinder and pressed the button.

"You can't take pictures of me in the tub!" she exclaimed. "I'm naked."

"You are surrounded by bubbles, and unfortunately, I can't see any of the good naked bits, so the photo is practically tame." Sebastian put the camera down and held out the box of macarons. "Here taste one."

Tess reached for the round chocolate delicacy filled with white crème. She took a bite and it melted in her mouth. "Oh my God," she moaned. "This is amazing." She had never eaten the sweet treat before and was grateful they didn't have a shop in New York. This honeymoon was going to make her fat.

Sebastian picked up the camera and started snapping more photos.

"Stop! It's bad enough you're taking the pictures of me naked. You need to get me eating, too?"

Sebastian stopped photographing Tess and knelt down beside her. "I'll stop if you share that macaron with me."

Tess smiled and then popped the rest of the treat in her mouth. Sebastian frowned, but Tess leaned over and kissed him, allowing his tongue to taste the chocolate and coconut. "Why don't you join me?"

Chapter 14 - This Summer

Paris

Bonjour from the City of Lights! Paris is a city full of culture and beauty. Sebastian and I are reveling in the lap of luxury at the George V. We spend our days scouring art galleries (the Musee D'Orsay was my favorite!), marveling at the architecture and eating croissants in quaint cafés. One of the highlights was the evening Sebastian took me to dinner at the Jules Verne restaurant at the top of the Eiffel Tower. The views, the food and having my husband by my side is a moment I'll remember forever.

Love you!

Tess

Monaco

Greetings from the municipality of Monaco! This is an amazing city on the sea. Sebastian and I spent our day lounging on Larvotto beach watching the rich and famous at play, and splashing in the clear blue Mediterranean Sea. In the evening, we got dressed up and went to the Casino de Monte-Carlo. I felt like I was in a James Bond movie and Sebastian looked so handsome in his tuxedo. He even won some money! Thank God, because you wouldn't believe how expensive it is to stay here.

Love you!

Tess

Barcelona

Hola! from Spain. Today Sebastian and I toured the basilica Sagrada Familia. I find it odd that Sebastian likes to tour churches but doesn't believe in religion. I love seeing the various architectural designs. Everything is so old in Europe compared to America. Sometimes I pinch myself to think I'm walking where someone walked a thousand years before me. We also visited the Picasso and Miró Museums. My favorite thing by far was the Barcelona Zoo. (Secretly, I think it was Sebastian's favorite, too!)

Love you!
Tess

Madrid

Greetings from Madrid, Madre! We visited the Royal Palace today. It's the largest palace in Western Europe. It was opulent, but I still prefer Buck House (Buckingham Palace). I guess my English husband is rubbing off on me. We strolled through the Plaza de Orienete and shopped in the local market. I wish you could be here with me to see all these wonders, but I'm happy I get to share them with you like this. I've taken so many photos, Sebastian made me mail them home so I wouldn't have to lug them around in my suitcase!

Miss you!

Tess

Rome

Ciao from Italy! The Vatican, the Sistine Chapel, and St. Peter's Basilica were amazing. Then of course exploring the ruins of the Colosseum and the Pantheon—so much history and better than any textbook I could read. The Trevi Fountain was magnificent. Sebastian and I threw a coin in the fountain. Legend has it that anyone who tosses a coin in the fountain will return to Rome someday. And the food—oh the food. Sebastian hasn't let me step foot into one McDonald's yet. (and I can't admit it to him, but I haven't minded at all!)

Love you!
Tess

Vienna

Servus from Vienna, Austria! I am in love with this city. From the old world baroque Schrobrunn Palace to the Lipizzan ballet, this city is full of wonder. Sebastian took me to see one of his favorite paintings, Gustav Klimt's "The Kiss." We had the most delicious sachertorte at Demel pastry shop. (I swear I've gained 10 pounds on this trip).

Love you!

Tess

Prague

Ajoj from Czechoslovakia! We walked through charming squares and crossed the city's many bridges, both ancient and modern, that span the Vltava River. The city is alive with Gothic architecture: soaring towers, spires, and buttresses. Sebastian and I attended a performance at the State Opera. I didn't understand a word the actors sang, but Sebastian was able to fill me in on the story.

Love you!

Tess

London

Greetings from jolly ole England! I can't believe how quickly these past two months have flown. As sad as I am to be ending this journey, I'm happy to be coming home to see my friends and family again. I'm so blessed to have Sebastian in my life. I definitely made the right decision in agreeing to marry him. I'm so happy, Mom. I hope to have a life full of love and happiness just like you and Dad. So many stops on this trip; so many memories. I can't wait to see you and tell you all about it in person and show you the photos I've taken on this trip.

See you soon!
Tess

Part 2 - Sophomore Year of College 1987

Chapter 15 - Into My Arms

Being back home in New Jersey and starting a new year at NYU left Sebastian with mixed emotions. Europe was so amazing because Tess was by his side. Although she was here with him now, there was something about not having a schedule and doing whatever he pleased that appealed to Sebastian. He definitely wanted to apply with Tess for the study abroad program, eager to explore more of Europe with her. Now all that was left was to decide on a city.

Tess was sitting on the couch studying. Suddenly she dropped her textbook on the floor and ran to the bathroom. Sebastian heard her retching behind the closed door. She slowly opened the door a few minutes later, looking a little worse for wear.

Sebastian handed her a cold glass of water. "Are you okay?"

"No, I feel so sick," she replied, the blood drained from her face.

"Are you pregnant?" he gingerly asked.

"How could I be pregnant?"

Sebastian gave her a quizzical look but said nothing. Tess punched him in the arm. "I mean, how could I be pregnant when I'm taking birth control?"

"Well, it's not a hundred percent effective, is it? How long have you been feeling like this?"

Tess did a quick mental calculation in her head and a look of sheer panic crossed her face. "I can't be pregnant," she reiterated with conviction.

"I'm running down to the pharmacy to get a pregnancy test." Sebastian grabbed his wallet and took the lift to the ground floor. Once outside, his mind wandered. Was it too much to hope that Tess might actually be pregnant? Even though he had never known his father, he could not dismiss the overwhelming desire he felt to be one. He wanted to give the baby everything he never had growing up. Sebastian wanted to share with his child all the wonderful things that Nanny had taught him. He made it to the pharmacy, just a few blocks away from the condo, and purchased the EPT. The female clerk gave him an odd look as she tucked the box in a small paper bag. Sebastian was grinning from ear to ear as he walked home with a boyish bounce in his step.

Tess grabbed the bag from Sebastian as soon as he entered the condo and ran back to the bathroom. She began to close the door behind her, but Sebastian placed his foot between the door and frame to stop her.

"What are you doing?" she asked while ripping off the box top.

"I'm waiting with you to see the results," he simply replied.

"Then turn around," she said, annoyed. "I'm nervous enough—I don't need you watching me pee on a stick."

Sebastian chuckled. He couldn't stop himself. "I've seen you naked and made love to you. You're really not going to be concerned with modesty now, are you?"

"Fine! Then you can read the directions," she huffed, tossing the piece of paper at him.

Sebastian began: "Remove the test stick from the foil packet…"

"Can you just cut to the chase," she growled.

"Yes, darling." He casually leaned back against the sink cabinet. "Pee on the stick and wait fifteen minutes. A plus signs means we're pregnant. A minus sign means we aren't." If Tess was this emotional now, how was Sebastian going to survive the next eight months if she were pregnant?

* * *

Tess peed on the stupid stick and placed it on the counter. Then she sat on the closed toilet lid and stared at the tile floor. She took the birth control pills religiously, never missing a day. They had been so careful—how could she be pregnant? She loved Sebastian with all her heart. She wanted to give him children, in ten years maybe, but not now. She still had three years of college to complete. How could she possible juggle a baby, a part-time job, and a full class load?

They waited an interminable fifteen minutes. She couldn't take her eyes off Sebastian's face as he picked up the stick to read the results. As hard as she wished for a negative outcome, in her heart she knew the test was positive. The smile on Sebastian's face only confirmed her suspicions.

"It's positive," he announced, showing her the test results.

She shook her head in dismay. "I can't do this, Sebastian."

He knelt down in front of her and took her hand. "Yes, you can. We can do this together. We have Henry and Alice and your mom." He chuckled to himself. "And Sigourney will spoil her rotten—although I don't see her changing any diapers."

"No…" she tried to protest, but he quieted her with a kiss.

"I love you. You've made me so happy, Tess. I know you value your independence and this is not fitting your timetable, but this baby is a blessing."

God, why did he always have to be right? What was wrong with her? She was about to give him the greatest gift she could give and all she felt was a ball of nerves, dread, and fear. All she could manage to say was, "I love you, too."

"You should see a doctor to confirm. These tests aren't always accurate. When we know for sure, we'll make plans. Will that make you feel better?"

She nodded her head in agreement and fell into his arms to be held. Right then all she needed was to be held by her husband.

* * *

A week later they were sitting in the doctor's office, listening to the doctor confirm the pregnancy. The baby was due at the end of April. They must have gotten pregnant that last night in London. Sebastian reminisced that it was a particularly good lovemaking session. He was over the moon; Tess was on the verge of tears. He escorted her out of the office and put her in the car; once inside, she wept freely. Sebastian offered her his handkerchief.

"Shh, don't be afraid. We're in this together," Sebastian tried to comfort her.

"You don't have to carry this child for eight more months, Sebastian."

"I would if I could, darling."

"I know," she sniffled, trying to calm down. "How am I going to do this? How can I go to class and keep my job?" She stopped for a moment, a look of realization crossing her face. "The semester abroad— that's out of the question now."

"Tess, they have hospitals overseas."

"I won't have this baby out of the country. I need my mom to be there when it's time."

Sebastian was silently relieved: at least Tess was going to have the baby. A small part of him feared she'd want to abort since this turn of events was most definitely not a part of her master timetable. He was so grateful she was willing to have the baby and he didn't have to sort out an argument to persuade her to keep the child.

"Okay, we'll stay here. There's no saying we can't study abroad our junior year instead."

"With a baby in tow?"

"We'll hire a nanny. I turned out all right being raised by one."

Tess took his hand. "I love you for trying to be so optimistic, but realistically, it won't happen. At least I had my grand adventure this summer," she said, full of melancholy.

Sebastian took her chin and turned her to face him. "Never give up on your dreams. It doesn't become you, Tess. You can have anything you want. You just have to believe."

"Please don't try to make me feel better. I'm confused. This is a huge, life-changing event that I'm not prepared for." She leaned her head back against the headrest and closed her eyes. "I want to give you this child. I know you'll be a fantastic father. I just can't wrap my mind around the fact that I'm going to have a baby in eight months."

"Do you want this child? All I hear you talk about is me and your willingness to give me this gift. If you're having second thoughts about bringing this baby into the world, I need to know about them now."

"Of course I'm having the baby—there is no other option for me. I'm just terrified about the whole experience. I don't know if I can handle it."

Sebastian leaned in and gently kissed her lips. "Don't underestimate yourself. You'll handle it like the strong person you are. Do you want to tell your mom?"

"No! It's too soon. I can't believe this is happening. How am I going to explain it to my mom? I'm only six weeks in. Let's wait until the second trimester, please?"

"Whatever you want, darling."

"I'm so tired. Can you please take me home? I need to sleep."

Sebastian turned the key in the ignition and drove toward home. Maybe she just needed time: time to get used to the idea of having a baby, time to adjust to the physical changes to her body. Maybe in time, she would become excited about the baby's impending arrival. All Sebastian could do was hope.

Chapter 16 - Earn Enough For Us

As the first trimester progressed, it was all Tess could do to get to class without throwing up on the subway or sidewalk. She was only two months into this journey, and she was so sick that she wished she could just lie down and die. Sebastian had been fretting over her and although he meant well, she just wanted to be left alone. She couldn't keep any food down and could barely drink water without that coming back up too.

Tess had given up her part-time job at the Strand, and when she wasn't studying, she was sleeping. Sebastian sat next to her drinking coffee in the cafeteria, but even the smell of the hot drink turned her stomach. "I've got to get out of here," she whispered, standing from the table. Then she blacked out.

* * *

Sebastian reacted quickly and caught Tess before she hit the floor. A few of the other students rushed over to help. They called an ambulance and took Tess to New York Hospital.

While the doctor examined her, Sebastian refused to leave the room, praying they didn't lose the baby. Tess was awake, but looked terrible: her body weak, dark circles under her eyes, and an ashen complexion.

"I'm happy to report everything is just fine," the doctor said.

"I don't feel fine," Tess replied wearily.

"You have hyperemesis gravidarum."

"English, please," Sebastian jumped in, annoyed at the doctor's nonchalant attitude.

"You have severe morning sickness. It's unusual, but it will do you no harm. I'll start an IV to get you fluids. You're dehydrated."

"How long do I have to stay here? I have classes."

"The classes can wait, Tess," Sebastian warned, taking hold of her hand.

"I'm going to keep you overnight and re-evaluate your progress in the morning." The doctor smiled down on Tess and then left the room.

"Thank God you're okay," Sebastian said, brushing the hair away from her face. "You had me so worried. Can we please call your mom now?"

"No, I don't want her dropping everything to rush up here. I don't want to worry her, Bas."

"Darling, I think it's a good idea for her to be here for you."

"Not yet. Can you please honor my wishes?" she pleaded. "I'll take it easy. You can wait on me hand and foot. I'll only leave the condo to attend class. Four more weeks and I'll be in my second trimester. I should be better by then and we can tell her at that time."

He sighed, placing his elbows on the hospital bed and looking into her eyes. "Fine, but I'm holding you to your word."

While he was waiting for the doctor to sign her release papers, he picked up a copy of *What to Expect When You're Expecting* in the gift shop. It wasn't for Tess, but for him to read. He had to get an understanding of what was going on in her head and what was happening to her body. When Sebastian brought Tess home from the hospital, he confined her to bed. He'd watch her round the clock if it kept her and the baby safe.

* * *

A week later, Tess was ready to strangle Sebastian. She knew he meant well, but his doting on her was suffocating. She couldn't take it any longer. "Sebastian, I'm not dying. Will you please leave me alone for a while? Go have a beer with Henry or go down to the gallery. I just need an evening alone!"

Looking like a wounded animal, he conceded and gave her some space. When he walked out the door, Tess let out a long, slow breath. She drew herself a hot bubble bath and enjoyed the peace and quiet. Her mind wandered back to their stay at the George V in Paris and the amazing clawfoot tub they spent many evenings in together. It wasn't so long ago, but how things had changed. She could feel her body changing. Soon, her clothes wouldn't fit anymore and she'd have to wear those awful tent dresses. Tess wasn't a fashion plate, but the thought of wearing maternity clothes made her cry.

She was emotional and felt as if she had no control over her life. Meanwhile, Sebastian was grinning like the happy bastard had just won the lottery. The baby should bring them together, but Tess felt it was pulling them apart.

* * *

Sebastian ended up downtown at the gallery. Fiona greeted him as he entered. "You're not scheduled today. What brings you in?"

"Tess kicked me out of the condo. She needed some *alone time*. I thought I'd pop in to see if you might be interested in me working more hours."

The gallery was empty, so Fiona motioned for him to join her on the leather sofa in the center of the sales floor. "Are you two having trouble in your marriage?"

"No, it's nothing like that at all." Sebastian hesitated, biting his bottom lip. He had kept the promise to keep quiet so far, but he was bursting to tell someone. Tess never came to the gallery, so he felt okay to share the news. "We're having a baby, Fiona."

"Congratulations! What wonderful news."

"It is wonderful news. It just wasn't planned and Tess is struggling to cope with the situation."

"So you're looking to make more money, with the baby coming."

"I actually have a few ideas in mind, but I wanted to talk to you first," Sebastian admitted.

"Let's make some tea and we'll talk," Fiona agreed.

Sebastian had a good visit with Fiona, and his plans were falling into place. Tess might still be in denial about their impending arrival, but Sebastian was bound and determined to have a plan in place to take care of his family.

When he walked into the condo, the lights were out. He quietly crept to the bedroom and opened the door. Tess was curled up in bed, fast asleep. She looked so beautiful and at peace. He stood there leaning against the doorframe and watched her for a while. Yes, he felt his plan would do nicely. Tess might not like it, but he'd deal with that later.

Chapter 17 - Mother's Talk

Sebastian and Tess drove home to Pennsylvania to have Thanksgiving dinner with Tess' mom. They entered the house and were greeted by the smell of a pumpkin pie baking in the oven.

Tess rushed over and hugged her mom, so happy to finally be home. The past few weeks, all she could think about was breaking the news to her mom. Tess hoped she would feel relief, with her mom's support, and could find some speck of happiness about the pregnancy.

"Hello, Kate," Sebastian said, handing over a large bouquet of autumnal flowers.

"They're beautiful. Come to the kitchen, dinner is almost ready."

After removing their coats, Sebastian placed them in the hall closet. He held Tess' hand and escorted her to the kitchen. "How can I help?" Sebastian asked as he pulled out a chair for Tess to sit down.

"I just need to carve the turkey. Would you like to do the honors?"

"Absolutely," Sebastian said as he took the carving knife from Tess' mom.

Kate busied herself placing various bowls of vegetables, stuffing, and cranberry sauce on the table. Sebastian finished carving the turkey and placed the platter on the table. They joined Tess at the table and tucked into dinner.

Thankfully, her morning sickness was subsiding. Tess was content to be back in her mom's kitchen, eating the best comfort food in the world. "This is so good, Mom."

"I'm glad to see your appetite return," Sebastian said.

"Have you been sick, Tess?"

Sebastian was grinning like a Cheshire cat, tapping his fork on the table. If it weren't so cute, Tess would be annoyed.

Tess' mom looked at Sebastian and then to Tess. Cocking her brow she said, "What's going on, you two?"

Tess took a deep breath and then announced, "I'm pregnant."

"We're having a baby!" Sebastian exclaimed.

It took a few seconds for the news to sink in. Kate titled her head, her lips curling up into a smile. "A baby."

"Are you pleased?" Tess wanted to know.

"Oh, honey—a baby. I'm going to be a grandmom!" Kate pushed away from the table and rushed over to Tess to give her a hug.

Sebastian stood from the table. "Can I get in on this?"

"Congratulations, Sebastian." She shook her head. "I'm surprised. I take it this wasn't planned."

Tess blushed with embarrassment. "Of course it wasn't planned. Do you think I want to take on NYU and an infant?"

"You'll be great," Sebastian reassured.

"You're my girl and you'll be a wonderful mom," Kate agreed.

"I'm kind of hungry, can we go back to eating?" Tess asked, wishing to stop talking about the baby. Talking about the baby made it real, and Tess wasn't ready to handle it. She didn't think she ever would be.

"When are you due?"

"The end of April," Sebastian answered. "Tess has had a bad bout of morning sickness and didn't want to say anything until she was in the second trimester."

"Tess, I'll take you shopping for maternity clothes tomorrow. Won't that be fun?" her mom asked.

"Tess looks fabulous, Kate. She doesn't need maternity clothes yet," Sebastian chimed in, knowing this was a sensitive subject for Tess. "We'll have to think about baby furniture."

"Oh, I still have Tess' cradle. I'll show you after dinner."

Tess let the two of them carry on with their discussion while she continued to enjoy her meal.

They were spending the night at Kate's home, so she gave up her bed for Sebastian and Tess. Kate slept upstairs in Tess' single bed.

"I think that went very well, don't you?" Sebastian asked as they lay in bed.

"Yeah, I guess."

"Did you really believe your mom would be upset?"

"No, she's always been supportive. I'm not surprised by her reaction."

"Tess, please talk to me. I feel like you're pulling away. I'm here to support you, but I don't know what you want me to do."

"I want you to stop talking about the baby. I don't want to go shopping with Mom for maternity clothes," she said, bursting into tears.

Sebastian pulled her close and held her in his arms. "You don't have to go shopping. How about we go the Philadelphia Museum of Art tomorrow instead?"

Tess let out a little hiccup as her tears subsided. "Yes, I'd like that. Maybe we can go to a nice restaurant in the city to celebrate my birthday, too."

"Now that's a brilliant idea."

"I just don't want to talk about the baby and I don't want any gifts that have to do with the baby. I just want to spend the day with you. I want things to go back to the way they were in Europe—just you and me wandering the city and enjoying spending time together."

"Whatever you wish, darling," Sebastian said while his hand stroked her hair.

The next morning, Sebastian rose from bed and joined Kate in the kitchen. He would let Tess sleep in because she needed her rest.

"Sebastian, would you like a cup of coffee?" Tess' mom asked while she sat at the table reading the newspaper.

"I'll get it," Sebastian responded, opening the cupboard to fetch a mug.

"I sense Tess isn't very excited about the baby," Kate said as he joined her at the table.

"That's an understatement," he sighed. "I know it wasn't planned, but I didn't think she'd react like this."

"Like what?"

"She's trying to ignore the fact that it's happening. She's told me she's happy to give me the baby, but I feel as if she's doing this for me and that if it were her choice, the outcome would be different. I offered her an out, told her if she wanted to have an abortion I'd support her, but she was adamant she would have the baby."

Kate reached over and took Sebastian's hand. "Tess could never do that. She doesn't believe in abortion. She loves you so much, I believe she wants to have the baby for you. I think her biggest fear is how does she care for a child and still have the career she's worked so hard for."

"I tried to convince her that she's not in this alone. Kate, I'll do anything for her and the baby. I've already been planning on what to do when the baby arrives."

"Have you discussed these plans with Tess yet? You're a procrastinator when it comes to sharing information with my daughter."

"The reason I procrastinate is because I assume she won't like the idea. I just want to do the right thing, but I feel as if I'm walking on eggshells with Tess. I've resorted to reading pregnancy books to try to figure out what's going on in that head of hers. Meanwhile, miss bookworm won't go near *What to Expect When You're Expecting*. I think she's in denial. I need your help to reach her. Maybe she needs a woman-to-woman conversation. Can you help me?"

"I'll see what I can do," Kate promised.

"Oh, and don't take her shopping for maternity clothes—she's not happy about gaining weight," Sebastian warned.

"We have our work cut out for us," Kate agreed.

Tess shuffled into the kitchen and grabbed a bottle of water from the refrigerator.

"Tess, do you want to go out for breakfast?" her mom asked.

"Sebastian and I were going to the art museum today."

"That's okay. You and your mom should spend some time together. Go to breakfast. I have some things I need to do and I'll make us reservations for dinner."

Tess gave him a wary glance.

Sebastian made a cross over his heart. "I swear I'll be good."

Tess and her mom sat in their favorite family restaurant eating eggs and toast.

"You're being unusually quiet this morning," her mom remarked. "How are classes at NYU?"

"They are good, but it's been a struggle this semester. I've been so tired and sick, it's been hard to keep up and concentrate on my studies. I hope now that the sickness has calmed down, I'll be able to get back to normal. We were going to do a study program abroad, but that won't happen now."

"Honey, Sebastian is worried about you. I am too. You don't seem to be yourself."

Tess placed her fork on her plate. "Mom, I love you both, but I'm really sick of everyone's concern. I'm angry, okay? I don't want to have this baby, not now, but it's too late for that. I just have to try and make the most of it." The comment made Kate speechless. Tess looked at her shocked expression and let out an audible sigh. "I'm sorry, it's just how I feel. I'm having this baby because it means so much to Sebastian, but I can't pretend to be happy about it. Do you think there is something wrong with me? Should I be seeing a therapist?" she asked, feeling confused and lost.

"Tess, pregnancy does weird things to a woman, both physically and emotionally. Other women have felt the same things you are feeling. The important thing is to talk about those feelings. I'm here anytime you want to talk, and Sebastian wants you to be honest about your feelings with him."

"You two have talked about this?"

"Yes, I'm glad he cares so much about you that he would share his concerns with me. I don't think you could have picked a better partner to marry."

"I know he was the right choice for me. I'm just not sure how to tell him all this without it coming out wrong—like I'm selfish and uncaring." Tess hung her head and shuddered. "The truth is I couldn't do any of this without his support."

"Then you need to tell Sebastian just want you told me."

Tess put her elbows on the table and laid her head in the palms of her hands. "How did you handle college and pregnancy when you and Dad found out you were having me?"

"We were thrilled when we found out we were having a baby. I was going to nursing school, so I already understood what was happening to my body from a medical standpoint. I guess that made it easier to accept. We wanted to have children at a young age. We hoped to have a whole house full of children. Of course that wasn't in the cards," her mom said with a tinge of melancholy.

"Maybe it was easier for you because you planned the pregnancy. I was on birth control and still got pregnant."

"You're not the first person that has ever happened to, Tess."

"I know. I'm sorry, I don't mean to be so ungrateful. I'm just trying to figure this all out."

"I know, honey. I'm always here for you."

* * *

Sebastian and Tess enjoyed their afternoon walking through the Philadelphia Museum of Art. He didn't talk about the baby; actually, he didn't talk much at all. Sebastian could sense Tess starting to relax, her shoulders loosening as the tension left her body. She was at his side, holding his hand, and it felt like old times.

He took her to Le Bec-Fin for her birthday dinner. It was extravagant, but Sebastian hadn't bought her a birthday present, so he figured Tess would forgive him for spending so much money on a meal. They dined on scrumptious French cuisine: foie gras, venison, grilled vegetables, and mouthwatering homemade bread.

Tess smiled as she took a bite of her venison. "This reminds me of Paris. I don't care how much it cost. Thank you for bringing me here tonight."

"It makes me so happy to hear you say that," he admitted, reaching over to caress her hand. "We'll get to Europe again, I promise."

"I miss seeing you in a suit," Tess admitted as she admired how handsome her husband looked sitting across from her. Then she leaned forward and whispered, "You look so sexy."

"I love you," he whispered back.

When their meal was consumed, the waiter brought a small birthday cake to the table. Tess' eyes lit up with joy. Sometimes it was so easy to make her happy. They each ate a piece of the chocolate dessert and had the remainder boxed to take home.

Tess held Sebastian's hand as they drove back to Kate's house. "Thank you, Bas. I needed a day like today—just you and me. The meal was incredible."

Sebastian chuckled. "So have I cured you of your McDonald's obsession?"

Tess laughed along. "No, I'll always have a special place in my heart for McDonald's, but I don't feel so out of place now when you take me to fancy restaurants."

"I'm glad to hear it," he said, stealing a glance at her as they headed down the expressway. "Happy birthday, Tess."

Chapter 18 - All I Want Is You

Sebastian cuddled with Tess on the sofa, the room lit by the fire roaring in the fireplace and the white twinkling lights of the Christmas tree. He was enjoying a piece of fruitcake Alice had made for him.

"I don't know how you eat that thing," Tess said, scrunching up her nose at the red and green candied fruitcake.

"It's delicious, but undoubtedly very English." He took a sip of coffee. "You know what I just realized? Next year at this time, we'll be celebrating the baby's first Christmas."

"The baby will only be eight months old. I doubt it will have any idea what is going on," Tess reasoned.

"Don't take all the fun out of this for me."

"Oh, I can totally see you staying up late on Christmas Eve putting together a bicycle."

"I won't do that. I'll pay someone at the store to put it together."

Tess laughed because it was typical Sebastian and one of the things she loved about him.

He stood and took his empty plate to the kitchen. Then Sebastian disappeared into the guest bedroom. He came back few minutes later holding a package. It was obviously a painting, Tess observed, looking at the eighteen-by-twenty-foot picture wrapped in Santa Claus gift wrap.

"We said we weren't going to buy each other any gifts this year," she reminded him.

"I didn't exactly buy it for you. It's for the baby."

"You're buying the baby art and it's not even born yet?"

"What makes you think it's art?" Sebastian asked.

"What else could it be, shaped like that? It's not a rocking horse."

She reached out and started to pull the paper off the frame. Inside was a bright yellow canvas with a black outline of a crawling infant.

The Keith Haring painting brought a smile to her face. The painting was fun and playful: perfect for a baby. She reached over and hugged her husband. "I love it, thank you. You didn't get it at the gallery, did you?"

"No, I stopped into the Pop Shop and had the chance to meet Mr. Haring. He made it especially for the baby. Turn the canvas around."

Tess looked on the back. There was an inscription in pencil. *For Baby Irons - K. Haring '87.*

"Please tell me it cost less than the Warhol."

"It cost much less than the Warhol, but that doesn't matter. I only care that you like it."

"I do," Tess reiterated. "Does this mean you'll be buying art for the baby every year as a Christmas gift?"

"That's an excellent idea. If I buy right, the baby may never have to work a day in her life."

He had that twinkle in his eye that told Tess she should have kept her mouth shut, but she couldn't be mad at him. His first investment had paid off and Sebastian had a good eye. He had the uncanny ability to pick the right art for investment's sake. Sebastian propped the painting against the coffee table and joined Tess on the sofa.

"You keep assuming it's a girl."

"It's just a hunch," Sebastian admitted.

"That's very scientific."

"We'll find out for sure when you have the ultrasound next week."

Tess lay on the examination table while the doctor prepared for her ultrasound. She held Sebastian's hand and they watched the black and white monitor. Suddenly they could see the outline: the baby's head and an arm stretched overhead.

"Look, she's waving." Sebastian grinned.

"And here is the heartbeat," the doctor pointed out.

Tess watched in amazement. Hearing and seeing the tiny heartbeat was overwhelming. It made the whole thing frighteningly real, and she wasn't sure whether to be thrilled or terrified.

The doctor continued moving the scanner over Tess' belly. "Everything looks good. Do you want to know the sex?"

"My husband is convinced it's a girl. Is he right?"

The doctor moved the scanner again to view another angle of the baby. "He's right. Congratulations, you're having a girl." The doctor cleaned the gel off Tess' stomach and removed his gloves. "I'll leave you alone for a few minutes."

Sebastian gazed down at Tess. "Did you hear that, darling? We're having a girl."

"Yes, it's wonderful news," she announced, trying to sound upbeat. "I'm so happy you're getting a little girl. You'll be an amazing father, Bas."

Thankfully, Sebastian was so enamored with the news that he didn't pick up on her anxiety, and simply stared at the frozen image of his daughter on the monitor.

They walked out into the cold wintery day after they finished at the doctor's office. "Hungry? Let's get an early dinner before we head home," Sebastian suggested.

"I'm always hungry," Tess frowned. Thank God for Lycra leggings and oversized sweaters. At least she was in fashion and hadn't had to buy dreaded maternity clothes yet.

"Where did you want to go?"

"The restaurant at Saks."

"Okay, shall we hail a taxi?" Sebastian inquired.

"No, I could use the exercise. Let's walk."

They crossed the street and continued up Fifth Avenue. "Are you happy we're having a girl?"

"I know you had your heart set on it. I'm glad you are getting what you want," Tess told him.

"I would love this baby no matter what sex it is."

Tess felt as if she was in a chokehold and couldn't breathe. She couldn't continue with this conversation. "How are things at the gallery? Anyone famous stop in lately?" she asked, attempting to change the subject.

"Things are going well. I have a client, Mrs. Irving, that wants me to find her the next big thing in London. She likes to purchase on the ground level so she can be the envy of all her friends."

"How do you do that?"

"Penny put me in contact with a few art dealers and I read the trades. It's all about connections and building relationships, though I must admit it would be easier if I could take a trip abroad to do it in person."

"You should do it. Maybe I could join you."

"And what about Mattie?"

There it was again: more talk about the baby. Only this time he was calling her by name. "Maybe my mom will take her for a week so we can go in the summer."

"I don't think I could leave her so soon. Can you?"

"I really don't know, Sebastian. I just don't want our lives to change because of the baby," Tess replied, feeling deflated.

Sebastian stopped walking and pulled Tess back against a building, out of the line of pedestrians, and into his arms. "Everything is going to change, Tess. It is inevitable. I know you're fighting it, but you need to prepare yourself."

"Couldn't we bring Alice along?" she asked in desperation. "Ever since we found out I was pregnant, things have changed between us. I just want my husband back. I want you all to myself, I don't care if it sounds selfish."

* * *

For the first time, Tess opened up to him about how she was truly feeling. He wasn't quite sure what to say in response. For the past several months she'd wanted to avoid conversations about Mattie, and now she had finally told him why. Sebastian never thought of the baby as a distraction, but maybe he had spent too much time thinking and talking about the impending arrival and less time doting on Tess. He felt a pang of regret. Of course she was in a fragile state, and he had done a poor job of making her feel loved and cherished.

"I'm yours, Tess—utterly and completely yours." He leaned in and kissed her with emotion. It must have been a good kiss, because he could hear a little moan of delight in the back of her throat.

"That's all I ever wanted, Bas."

They ate an early supper at Saks and then Sebastian took Tess to a movie. They shared a bucket of popcorn and Sebastian had his arm around his wife throughout the film. She snuggled into him, a happy expression on her face. She didn't even seem to mind that he'd dragged her to another John Hughes movie. They were together and he was focusing his attention on her.

She leaned into him and whispered, "Thank you."

Chapter 19 - Love Plus One

Tess was well into her second trimester, but rarely talked to Sebastian about the pregnancy. He pampered Tess and gave her love and attention. Things were great between them if the baby was left out of the conversation. However, not talking about the baby was increasingly difficult for Sebastian. Where he would spend his time reading pregnancy books, Tess dove deeper into her coursework. No matter how he tried to reach her, they were drifting further apart. It was killing him and he didn't understand why she couldn't be happy like he was. Sometimes he felt like giving up and getting off the emotional roller coaster she had put him on, but he loved her too much to ever consider walking away.

It was Saturday evening and both Tess and Sebastian were sitting on the sofa. Tess was studying, Sebastian was reading a novel. He had to say something; the silence was killing him. Gently closing her textbook and removing it from Tess' grasp, Sebastian said, "We need to talk."

"About what?"

"The baby."

"We always talk about the baby," she said in exasperation.

"That's not true, Tess. You're in denial. The baby is coming whether you want it or not."

"Yes, I know that, Bas. I'm the one who has gained fifteen pounds and can't fit into her clothes anymore. Don't try to pretend you know what I'm going through," she warned in anger.

"I think I do know what you're going through. I'm the one reading the books," Sebastian countered, holding up the pregnancy book that was sitting on the coffee table.

"Books are fine in theory, but reality is very different. I knew the first year of marriage was going to be a challenge, but I wasn't expecting to be pregnant, too. I can't raise a baby and graduate at the top of my class and become a journalist. I don't want to sacrifice my dream," Tess ground out.

"I never asked you to give up your dream, and you don't have to. I have a plan." Sebastian took her fingers in his hands. He took a deep breath and prayed she didn't go mental on him when he uttered the next sentence. "I'm not going back to NYU in the fall. I'm staying home to raise the baby, so you can graduate and get a job. You already made my dream come true by marrying me and giving me this child. I finally have the family I've always wanted. I'm so grateful that I had Nanny Jones, but I won't dump my child off on a governess. I hope you understand my logic behind this."

Tess was dumbstruck. She stared at him for the longest moment, trying to come to grips with what he had just told her. So many things ran through her mind, and they all led back to the same conclusion. It seemed like the perfect solution for them both. Tess was terrified to become a mother and had no faith she could do a good job. She had even contemplated asking Sebastian if they could hire Alice to become a full-time nanny. The idea of Sebastian staying home to care for the child put her at ease. She might be ill equipped to be a mother, but she had absolutely no qualms that Sebastian would make an excellent father.

Sebastian was right to want to raise the child. He had a terrible relationship with his mother, which had disintegrated beyond repair, and a nonexistent relationship with his father. Tess had a good upbringing and wanted that for their child. She only wished she could love the baby half as much as Sebastian already did. Maybe that love would come in time—once the baby was born. Right now it was just a foreign object taking residence in her body. She was having a difficult time thinking of the baby as a human being, even after seeing the sonogram in the doctor's office.

"You're right. I think it's the best solution," she calmly stated.

"Really?"

"I know you'll take good care of us both. Will you keep your job at the gallery? You've done so well there and we could use the extra money with another mouth to feed."

Sebastian grinned and leaned in to kiss her on the lips. "Yes, I'm staying at the gallery. Fiona can give me more hours and Alice offered to babysit on the days I have to go into the city." He paused and looked into her eyes. "You're really on board with this?"

"I'm all in. We can do this, right?"

"Absolutely."

Tess turned on the sofa and placed her feet on Sebastian's lap. "Rub my feet, please."

He complied without complaint, rubbing her feet with his knuckles. It felt so good, she lay back on the couch and closed her eyes, and maybe for the first time in months she felt some relief. Sebastian would take care of them; she knew it in her heart—she just needed to keep reminding her brain of that fact.

"How am I doing?" Sebastian asked.

"Perfect," she murmured, her eyes still closed. Suddenly she felt a spasm in her belly—the baby kick for the first time. Her eyes flew open and her hand reached over her abdomen.

"What is it?" Sebastian anxiously questioned.

Tess stilled and then began to smile. "The baby is kicking." She grabbed his hand and placed it on her belly.

Sebastian's expression turned to awe. "Oh my God, that's amazing." He leaned down and said to Tess' stomach, "You're going to be a strong one, like your mummy, aren't you?"

"I'm sure she can't understand a word you're saying."

"Yes, she can. It's in the book. You really should read it. I've been marking passages for you." Sebastian grabbed the book and handed it to his wife.

Tess rolled her eyes but accepted the book. As much as she wanted to hide, feeling the baby move inside her flipped some kind of invisible switch in her brain. She needed to prepare for what was to come, for it seemed Sebastian was far more versed in what to expect than she was.

In that moment she felt close to her husband—closer than she had for some time. "I'd like to go to bed," she said as she sat up.

"Okay, I'll be in shortly," he replied.

Tess gave him her sexiest grin. "Don't be daft, Bas. I'd like you to take me to bed, and I don't want to sleep."

"Oh. In that case, let me assist you." Sebastian smiled as he picked her up off the couch and carried her to the bedroom. "You know it kind of turns me on when you call me Bas."

"Yes, I know," she said, placing her arms around his neck.

* * *

After four months of waiting, she finally wanted to make love. It had been so long, the invitation had gone right over his head. Thank God he had been reading up on pregnancy. As much as he longed to be with her sexually, he didn't want to hurt her or the baby. He had plenty of ideas on how to make their foray enjoyable for Tess.

She may have been worried about her weight gain, but Sebastian believed he had never seen her look more voluptuous. Her breasts were fuller, her curves more pronounced; it really was true what they say about a pregnant woman glowing. He kissed her swollen belly and ran his hands over her soft skin.

Their lovemaking was slow and sensual. He took his time, wanting to savor being with Tess again. Watching her atop him moving back and forth, gloriously naked, made him come undone.

They lay in each other's arms, awash in bliss. "What does it feel like when you're inside me?" Tess asked.

He didn't expect that question, so he said the first thing that came to mind. "Beautiful." He looked over to see her expression. She was crying. "Oh no, did I say something wrong?"

She furiously shook her head. "No, you said everything right. I love you, Bas."

They kissed, a lazy, slow kiss that made his body tingle and his heart sing. "I love you, Tess. I've missed this so much."

They didn't talk anymore; they merely enjoyed their intimacy and fell to sleep in each other's arms.

In the morning Sebastian brought Tess breakfast in bed. They read the Sunday paper and lounged in bed until noon.

"We should shower. What would you like to do today?" Sebastian asked.

"I want to stay in bed all day."

"Hmm, you might be able to persuade me," he replied, sneaking a kiss on her neck. "You're not going to study today?"

"No, I need a break. I've neglected you for too long. I'm sorry. I didn't mean to. It's just everything has been so crazy."

"I know, darling. Life just happens sometimes. We need to promise each other that we'll never let it get in the way of our relationship. Promise me we'll always make time for one another, whether it is due to class, or work, or the baby."

"I promise," she vowed, snuggling into his body.

While Tess was in class, Sebastian met up with Sigourney at Bloomingdale's.

"What can Auntie Sigourney help you with today?" she asked, perusing the lunch menu in the café.

"You have to help me pick out some clothes for Tess. She refuses to buy maternity clothes and all she wears are leggings and oversized sweaters. I can't help but think that if she has something nice to wear, she'll feel better about herself."

Sigourney pondered his request. "Why don't you just buy her a few wrap dresses? All you have to do is buy her a bigger size."

Sebastian grinned. "You're brilliant!"

"Yes, I know," she replied without an ounce of modesty. "And go up half a size on the shoes. That should work nicely." Sigourney closed the menu and looked at her brother. "How is Tess doing? I know she's had a rough go of it."

"That's putting it mildly." Sebastian frowned. "She's afraid to have the baby. Afraid that everything will change between us. I know it's hormonal, but I just don't know how to convince her we'll be okay. I feel like I'm walking a tightrope, never quite sure what frame of mind Tess in is on any given day. I want my strong, confident, fearless Tess back."

"Maybe once the baby is born, things will get back to normal," Sigourney offered.

"Maybe."

"Will you let me give her a baby shower?"

"I don't know if that's a great idea. Remember what happened the last time you threw her a shower?"

"It doesn't have to be at the brownstone. We can have it at the condo. The baby needs furniture, clothes, accessories."

Sebastian laughed. "Accessories—you make it sound like she'll be draped in jewels and handbags."

"No, silly—I mean bottles, pacifiers, nappies."

"I know she needs all those things, but right now I'm just trying to keep Tess happy. I reckon I could use your help putting something small together."

Sigourney grinned. "I'm on it!"

Sebastian chuckled. "Honestly, sometimes I think you would have made a better party planner than a pianist."

"I can't help I love a good party. Neither can you—admit it."

"I do love a good party," he admitted. "Will you call the guests and arrange a catered luncheon?"

"Done!"

The baby shower went off without a hitch—at least Sebastian thought it did. Tess was smiling and appreciative of the many gifts the baby received. They now had furniture, a pram, a playpen, clothing, and—as Sigourney put it—lots of accessories. All they needed was the baby.

"It was a nice party, wasn't it?" Sebastian asked Tess as they sat on the sofa, alone, surrounded by gifts.

"Yes, it was nice. I knew you and your sister wouldn't let me get away without a shower. She did an amazing job, as always. I was just thankful Lily didn't show up this time." Tess slowly shook her head. "Look at all this stuff. We're going to need a bigger place to live."

"The gifts aren't frivolous. We needed everything we received."

Tess looked at Sebastian, raising her eyebrows.

"Well, we didn't need the silver rattle from Tiffany, but I had to buy it."

"You should have bought her a silver spoon," Tess teased.

"I'll lavish you both, if you let me," Sebastian said in all honesty.

"In due time." Tess winced as she arched her back and placed her hand behind her to rub the sore spot. Sebastian took over, giving her a massage to ease her aches and pains. "I hope this baby comes soon. I'm so uncomfortable."

"It won't be long now," he reassured her.

"Thank you."

He didn't respond, he merely kissed the top of her head and continued rubbing her back.

Chapter 20 - Our Day

On April 21, 1987, Martha Katherine Irons was born at 3:24 p.m., weighing in at seven pounds, two ounces. She was seventeen inches long. Proud papa Sebastian was beaming as he cradled the infant in his arms. He had never felt such satisfaction or overwhelming love. How he could have created such an exquisite human being, he could not fathom. "She's beautiful, just like you," he told Tess as she rested in the hospital bed.

"I'm exhausted. I need to sleep."

The nurse walked over to Sebastian and took the baby. "We'll bring her back in a few hours for her feeding."

Sebastian pulled a chair up next to the bed and took Tess' hand. "You get some rest. I'll be right here with you."

Tess squeezed his hand and then drifted off to sleep.

Kate walked into the room shortly thereafter. "How's she doing?" she whispered.

"Good, she's just tired."

"When was the last time you ate?"

Sebastian tried to recall. "Maybe breakfast yesterday?"

"Okay, you know how Tess sleeps. Go get yourself something to eat. I'll stay here with her."

"Thank you," he gratefully accepted.

Sebastian was in desperate need of coffee and anything to stop his grumbling stomach. He left the hospital and found a corner café, where he ordered up the biggest breakfast they had on the menu.

He ravenously tucked into the pancakes, eggs, and bacon. Sebastian had to ring Sigourney and tell her the good news. He could have hiked Uptown to deliver the news in person, but he didn't want to be away from the hospital for too long. Sebastian couldn't wipe the silly grin from his face. He was a father. It was the best high he had ever experienced, and that was saying something considering the way he had lived his life in the past.

After he finished eating, he left a generous tip for the waitress and then stopped at the flower shop and picked a bouquet of pink roses for Tess. When he got back to the hospital, he headed for the maternity ward to peek in on Mattie. She was sound asleep, bundled in a blanket and wearing a pink hat on her head.

Tess was still sleeping when he returned to her room. He set the vase of flowers on the side table and stood behind Kate, who was seated next to the bed. The nurse came back in the room with Mattie, who was crying. The sound woke Tess from her sleep.

"Ready to try breastfeeding?" the nurse asked, handing the infant to Tess.

"No, I want to bottle feed."

"Are you sure? It's such a good way to bond with the baby. The health benefits are outstanding."

Tess looked at Sebastian and he could read the anxiety in her eyes. "Give the baby to me and please bring a bottle. My wife doesn't want to breastfeed."

The nurse did as requested and quickly left the room to fetch a bottle.

Tess let out the breath she had been holding. "Thank you, Sebastian."

Kate sat down on the corner of the bed next to her daughter. "If you want to bottle feed that's perfectly acceptable. It might be a better solution since you'll be going to class everyday and Sebastian will be home with Mattie."

Tess slowly nodded her head in agreement, but didn't say a word.

* * *

Tess watched Sebastian as he fed Mattie her bottle. The infant nuzzled into him, as if instinctively knowing he would protect her for the rest of her life. Tess wondered if that was where the term "wrapped around her little finger" came from. Sebastian was happy: smiling, cooing, and fussing over his baby daughter. Tess had never seen him so blissful, not even with her. Was it possible that he loved the baby more than he loved Tess?

Sebastian looked up at Tess. "Do you want to feed her?"

"No, you finish."

"I brought you roses," he said, motioning to the bedside table.

Tess looked over at them and smiled. "They're so pretty. Thank you."

* * *

Kate stayed at the condo with Tess and Sebastian the first week after the baby was born. Mattie was born on a Monday and Tess was back at NYU by Wednesday. A part of Sebastian was happy to have her out of the house because he could spend some time with Kate and pick her brain. She was a pediatric nurse, after all, so maybe Kate could shed some light on why Tess was acting so distant.

"Kate, I've been reading up on postpartum blues. Do you think that's what's happening to Tess? I just thought that maybe once Mattie was born, she'd look into her eyes and fall in love, but it seems as if she couldn't wait to get out of the house and away from us."

"If it is the blues, it could last up to a few weeks. It's not unusual for a woman to experience it, especially after the birth of her first child."

"I understand her body is going through changes, but I don't feel anxious and moody. I've never been happier and I'm now responsible for a family. Shouldn't I be upset?"

"I think you're so happy because deep down, this is what you always wanted—a family to love. I'm grateful that you and Tess ended up together. I couldn't have asked for a better partner for her." Kate sat down on the sofa and gazed out over the Hudson

River. "Tess was anxious and lost when her dad died. Once she decided to throw herself into her schoolwork, she leveled out. I think we just need to give it some time."

"There's only a few more weeks left of school. What happens when the summer arrives and there's no schoolwork to distract her? What happens when she has to face this head-on? She's the strongest person I know, and seeing her suffer like this, I wish I knew what to do," Sebastian admitted, frowning.

Kate looked at Sebastian, her brow creased with worry. "We'll keep an eye on her together."

Just then the baby began to cry. "I'll get her," Kate said, standing up from the couch.

Sebastian remained behind, so many thoughts running through his brain. He wasn't a religious man, but he prayed that Tess would come around. It seemed unfathomable that their relationship could shift like this—Sebastian the strong personality who was responsible and nurturing, Tess the scatterbrain who was fleeing responsibility. They had completely changed roles, and it unnerved him. Sitting there worrying about it wasn't going to change anything, so he stood up and walked over to the guest bedroom and peeked inside. Grandmom Kate was sitting on the rocking chair, whispering to Mattie. He couldn't make out exactly what she was saying, but the smile on Kate's face was priceless.

* * *

Tess sat in the NYU library and enjoyed the silence it gave her. There was no crying baby, no hovering mother or doting husband to interrupt her peace. They didn't want her to go back to school so soon after the birth, but what else could she do? Exams were coming up next week and she needed to push to finish out the year with a respectful GPA. She'd already blown the 4.0 due to the extreme sickness and exhaustion during her pregnancy. She'd be damned if she wasn't going to give it her all and see if she could salvage her grades. If Sebastian couldn't understand that, then that was his problem, not hers. Right now Tess could only handle one thing, and that was school. The baby was in very capable hands and certainly didn't need a basket-case mother to try and take care of her.

When Tess arrived home, Sebastian was making dinner and her mom was reading a magazine. "Hi," she greeted as she entered the condo.

"Hello darling, how was your day?"

"Good. I was able to get a decent cram session in at the library. How was your day? Were you able to get any studying in?"

"No, not today." He looked up from the stove and continued, "Don't worry, I'll be ready to take my exams next week. All I have to do is pass so I get the credits for the course."

Tess wanted to argue, but decided against it. "Okay, as long as you get the credits. You might want to go back and get your degree someday."

Sebastian smiled at his wife. "Agreed. Now both you ladies come sit, dinner is ready."

They took their seats and Sebastian served up a meal of grilled chicken with a baked potatoes and broccoli. "Sebastian, you've become quite the cook," Kate complimented.

"Thank you."

"Mom, I'm so happy you were able to take the week off work and stay with us. I'm sorry I didn't thank you earlier."

"Well, you were a little busy having a baby, honey."

"I hope you're imparting tons of tips to Sebastian."

"Sebastian is a natural."

Tess laughed aloud. It seemed impossible that the wealthy bad boy she had met three years ago had left that image behind to become a committed, loving spouse and father.

"What's so funny? Is it that hard to believe?" Sebastian interrupted.

"I'm amused because we seemed to have switched places. I expect you to give me a calendar with schedules and time tables."

He cracked a smile. "I just might do that."

* * *

It was an idea he hadn't contemplated. Maybe the way to approach motherhood was to put it in terms Tess could understand and get excited about. The epiphany appeared and Sebastian finally felt a glimmer of hope.

He was humming a little tune to himself and as he loaded the dishwasher after dinner. Tess and Kate were watching TV in the living room and he wanted to give them some alone time. He prepared Mattie's bottle and then went to the bedroom to feed her.

As Mattie's tiny hands latched onto the bottom of the bottle and she began to drink, Sebastian marveled at his small miracle. She had a cute button nose, just like her mum, and deep blue eyes like her dad.

Brushing back the small tuft of brown hair that grew atop her head, he smiled. "I'm formulating a plan, Mattie. I'm enlisting Grandmom Kate to help. Mum will come around, I promise."

The baby cooed in his arms. Tess would come to love this baby, he just needed to find the right trigger to get her emotionally involved, and he thought he just might have found it.

At the end of the week, Kate went back to Pennsylvania. Tess was attending classes, but Sebastian remained home with Mattie. All he had to do was read over the class notes and take his finals. He only needed to pass; he wasn't concerned with his GPA, like Tess. He was quite proficient with nappie changing and bottle feeding. Although he had no idea what Mattie's cries meant, he was instinctively finding his way. He couldn't wait to complete his few last exams this week, so he could be finished with school altogether. He had far more pressing issues to deal with than classes.

Mattie loved music, whether it was playing on the TV, coming from the radio, or Sebastian was singing to her. He was happy to introduce her to something he loved so much—although she didn't understand a word of the lyrics.

He had just finished feeding Mattie her bottle and put her against his shoulder to burp her. After a few gentle taps on the back, the little girl belched and Sebastian felt something wet on his shoulder. "Oh, Mattie!" he exclaimed, and then silently cursed himself for forgetting to place a cloth over his shoulder.

Sebastian laid the infant in her playpen and stripped off his lightweight cashmere sweater. There was a knock at the front door. He walked over and opened the door to find Alice standing in the hallway. He stepped aside to allow her entrance.

"Are you okay?" she asked.

"Mattie just spit up on my cashmere," Sebastian lamented.

Alice took the sweater from him, grimacing at the sour smell. "A little baby shampoo and a cold water soaking should do the trick."

"Alice, you are an angel," Sebastian said, leaning down to kiss her cheek.

Alice simply chuckled. "Just do me a favor: don't wear anything that should be dry cleaned for the next two years—at least when you're around the baby."

"Okay—jeans and T-shirts. Tess will love that," he muttered. Sebastian sat at the breakfast bar talking with Alice while she worked on getting the stain out of his sweater.

"You seem to handling fatherhood very well."

"I've never been happier, Alice."

"I can tell. Whatever happened to that petulant young man who showed up on the steps of Edgewood smoking cigarettes and demanding scotch?"

He chuckled. "That seems like a lifetime ago. I'm a changed man. Blame it on my girls."

"I don't think you give yourself enough credit. You changed yourself, Tess didn't force you. You're a good man, Sebastian."

Chapter 21 - My Baby

Sophomore year was over, and Tess ended up with a 3.8 GPA. She wasn't thrilled with the results, but all things considered, she could have done much worse. Now she was faced with spending the next two and a half months with the baby while Sebastian worked at the gallery.

"So tomorrow is the big day," he said as he cleared the dishes from the table.

"Don't remind me. You called Alice in as my reinforcement, right?"

"Yes, I put her on notice. I'll only be working for six hours."

Tess shook her head in doubt, her eyes full of worry. Sebastian raced up to the loft and came back holding a piece of paper. He sat back down at the table next to Tess and began. "I have a schedule for you."

Tess looked down at the spreadsheet, each hour giving meticulous notes. "What is a nappie?"

"A diaper," Sebastian explained.

"Then why didn't you just say diaper?"

"I thought you loved my British slang. I was hoping to make this fun for you." Sebastian caressed the side of her face. "Admit it, you love lists and schedules."

Although a part of her wanted to be annoyed, Tess was relieved. Maybe this is what she needed—structure and a plan. If she approached her classes this way and that always worked out for her, maybe applying the same technique to childrearing would work as well. Tess looked him in the eyes and smiled. "I do love it. If there is any way for me to become comfortable with caring for a baby, I guess this would be it."

* * *

Sebastian leaned down and kissed Tess' lips. It was a sweet, innocent kiss. All the spark and passion of their relationship was missing. He chalked it up to the hormonal changes in her body. He understood the depression she was struggling with, yet he sorely missed being intimate with his wife. The doctor recommended waiting six weeks after childbirth, but

Sebastian hadn't been with Tess for two months leading up to the birth and his patience was wearing thin. Of course, he couldn't tell her how he was feeling. She had too much to deal with already and he wouldn't put any more undue pressure on her.

"I think you'll be a natural at this," Sebastian tried to reassure her. "Just look at how wonderful you are with being organized and bossing people around."

"Bossing people around?" she asked with ridicule.

"Well, maybe just bossing *me* around, which I secretly love." He grinned.

She gave him a small smile and stood from the table. "Will you hold me?"

Sebastian wrapped his arms around Tess and gently kissed her forehead. "Mattie sleeps most of the day anyway. Try to enjoy your day—maybe read a novel. You'll be brilliant, darling."

"And if I'm not?"

"You are not a quitter. Failure isn't in your vocabulary."

Tess took a deep breath and slowly let it go. "Alice will be here if I call her?"

"Yes, she'll be popping in while I'm out."

"Okay, I can do this," she said in a shaky voice.

Sebastian had a feeling she was trying to convince herself more than she was trying to convince him. As hard as this was for him, he had to walk away and leave her to it. It would be the only way she would bond with Mattie.

* * *

It took a while for Tess to fall asleep that night, her head on Sebastian's chest listening to his steady, strong heartbeat. He had faith that she could do this, so why didn't she? She had been sad and lonely since Mattie's birth. Knowing it was normal for a woman to feel that way didn't bring her any comfort. She was weepy and scatterbrained; gone was the strong girl who was on top of everything. Most of all, she missed being with Sebastian—making love with him. Would she ever get her sexual desire back?

Mattie's cry woke her at 3 a.m., but before she could put her foot on the floor, Sebastian was up and heading to the other room. Tess laid her head back on the pillow and closed her eyes. She listened as Sebastian prepared the bottle and then silence fell as he fed Mattie. She slipped out of bed and crept into the living room. She watched as Sebastian rocked Mattie back and forth in front of the window. He was singing very softly to the baby, and it melted Tess' heart to see him like this—the perfect father.

"What are you singing?" she whispered, walking up behind him and touching his shoulder.

"*Asleep* by The Smiths."

"That's a rather sad song for an infant."

"Yes, I know, but she likes the melody."

"So you're giving our daughter a crash course in British New Wave music?" Tess chuckled.

"Absolutely."

The bottle was empty and Sebastian stood from the rocking chair, ready to take Mattie back to her crib.

"Here, let me do it," Tess said, extending her arms.

Sebastian smiled as he carefully handed Mattie over to Tess. She cradled the infant in her arms and walked to the bedroom. Tess slowly put her daughter into the crib and placed the blanket over her. The baby tucked her tiny, curled-up fist under her chin, happy with a full tummy.

"See? You're a natural," Sebastian complimented as he placed his arm around Tess' waist and steered her back to their bedroom.

The alarm went off at 8 a.m. Sebastian proceeded to shower and ready himself for the day. He joined Tess in the kitchen, dressed in a suit and tie. She handed him a cup of coffee.

"Alice will be stopping by. If you need anything, call me at the gallery."

"I will," Tess agreed.

Sebastian kissed her on the lips. "I love you. Have a good day."

"I love you, too."

With that he was out the door, leaving Tess all alone with Mattie. Tess got a quick shower and dressed in a pair of shorts and a tee shirt. As she brushed her hair back into a ponytail, she heard Mattie's cries from the other room.

She walked toward the crib with quick, brisk strides, determined to conquer her fear. She warily eyed the infant and gave herself a silent pep talk. Then she picked up the baby and rocked her back and forth. "What's wrong, Mattie?"

She didn't actually expect Mattie to respond, and didn't need her to. She could smell what was wrong. "Okay, time to change this diaper."

Tess laid the infant on the changing table and went to work, wiping, powdering, and securing the diaper. Thank God for disposable diapers; she didn't think she could stomach washing out a cloth diaper like her mom had to years ago.

The clean diaper didn't make Mattie happy, and she continued to cry. Tess picked her up and walked into the living room. She took a seat in the rocking chair and tried to calm the fussy infant. First she held the baby close to her, Mattie's head resting on Tess' shoulder. "Mattie, I can't sing to you like your father. I wish you could tell me what you want. Your father left me a schedule and you're not due to eat for another half an hour."

As if Mattie could understand, she cried even louder. "Okay, well maybe we can dispense with the schedule. Oh, if Bas heard me say that he'd be on the floor howling in a fit of laughter."

Tess placed the baby back in the crib and made her way to the kitchen to warm up a bottle. There was knock on the door. Thank goodness Alice was here. "It's open," Tess called.

"How's it going?" Alice asked, walking through the front door.

Mattie wailed from the other room. "I'm going to try and feed her. I don't know what else to do," Tess said, feeling helpless.

"I'll go fetch her."

Alice walked into the bedroom and picked up Mattie. Instantly, she ceased crying.

Tess looked at Alice in awe. "How did you do that?"

"I thinks she prefers to be held like this. She doesn't want to miss anything," Alice replied holding the baby's back again her chest with her arm under Mattie's legs so the baby had a full view of what was happening.

Tess sat in the rocker and Alice handed Mattie over to her. Mattie took the bottle without hesitation and finally calmed down. Tess felt relieved.

"You've got this," Alice reassured. "How about I make us some lunch?"

"Oh, I would love that. Thank you, Alice."

Tess gently rocked back and forth. Mattie was happy, Alice was here as backup, and Tess was doing okay. When Mattie finished the bottle, she started to fuss. Tess sat the baby on her lap so she could look out the window and rubbed her back in an attempt to burp her. That wasn't working, so she tried a few gentle taps on the back. The baby burped and stopped whining, and then nestled back against Tess' stomach. Alice was onto something: it seemed that as long as Mattie could watch what was going on around her, she was content.

Tess felt Mattie fall asleep in her arms and carefully took her back to her crib. She and Alice sat down to eat lunch.

"Thanks for the tip, earlier. Do you have any others to impart?" Tess asked. "This instant mom thing is freaking me out."

"Every baby is different. You'll get to know her, discover what she likes. What an amazing time this is for you."

"I'm scared out of my mind, Alice. I'm responsible for another human being who is completely helpless and defenseless."

"Well, if you continue to think about it in those terms, you'll drive yourself insane."

"Tell me about it," Tess muttered under her breath. "Sebastian seems so much more comfortable with the whole idea of parenthood than I am."

Alice smiled. "That man loves you two so fiercely. He's made quite the turnaround since the first time I met him."

Tess took a bite of her salad. *Yes, he is amazing.* "I'm so lucky he chose me, Alice."

"I think Sebastian sees it the other way around."

"Maybe it's just fate. All I know is that I couldn't have had this baby without him."

Chapter 22 - Just Like Heaven

Sebastian walked through the front door of the condo, his face hidden by a large bouquet of summer flowers.

"Welcome home!" Tess said, running to him and all but jumping into his arms.

"I missed you, too," he said. "How was your day with Mattie?"

"We both survived."

"As I knew you would." Sebastian handed Tess the flowers. "I bought these for you."

"Thanks, I'll put them in some water."

"Let me get out of the suit and check on Mattie," he said, giving Tess a quick kiss on the lips.

Sebastian made his way to check in on his daughter first. She was sound asleep—his little angel. Then he changed out of his suit and into a pair of jeans and polo shirt. He was so relieved to come home to a happy wife and baby. He honestly didn't know what he would have done if he'd come home to find Tess dissolved in a puddle of tears. Things were progressing well.

When he joined Tess in the living room, she handed him a scotch. Sitting on the sofa next to her, he put his arm around her shoulders. "I'm proud of you, darling."

"Your schedule helped and so did Alice."

"Good. So you have no more qualms about being here without me when I have to go to work?"

"I wouldn't go that far," Tess snickered. "And I don't think you should refer to the gallery as work."

He wasn't quite sure what she met by that comment and gave her a quizzical glance. "That's what it is, isn't it?"

"Essentially, yes—but it's your passion. Work seems like something you're forced to do. You aren't forced to spend time there. You love it."

Sebastian had never thought of it in those terms. Tess was correct: it was his passion. The time he spent in the gallery seemed to speed by and before he knew it, it was time to come home to his family. How on earth had be become so lucky to have this life? The funny thing was that most people wouldn't consider being stripped of their birthright and losing their inheritance a blessing, but not Sebastian. He had never been happier.

"Have I told you lately how spectacular you are?"

She looked up at his face and smiled. "Actually, I don't think you have ever called me spectacular, and I certainly don't feel that great right now."

"What are you talking about?"

"Look at me, Bas. I'm an overweight, emotional wreck."

Sebastian placed his glass on the coffee table and turned to face Tess. "Stop—I love you and I think your weight is perfect." He loved the extra fullness of her curves and her buxom breasts, but he knew better than to try to verbalize it lest he screw it up and it came out all wrong. "I miss being intimate with you."

Tess frowned. "I'm sorry. I just haven't felt up to it."

"Shh, don't apologize. I understand. I just wanted you to know how much I desire you."

Tess wrapped her arms around her husband and leaned her head on his shoulder.

"I want to do something special for you?"

"What did you have in mind?" Tess asked in a leery voice.

"I want you to be pampered. After everything you've gone through this past year, you deserve it. I'm sending you to the spa."

"What?"

"I want you to have a day of solitude. You can have a massage and a facial, relax in the whirlpool, and have your hair and makeup done. All while surrounded by a peaceful luxury. It will be just like spending the day at the library," he said with excitement.

"I don't see how that is remotely anything like spending the day at the library, but I do admit, I feel like I could use some pampering."

"Excellent. I'll set it up."

"Have you talked to Fiona about the trip to London?" she asked, her heart filled with hope.

"You really want to go, don't you?"

"Yes. Maybe it will help me feel normal again. You know I've been depressed since Mattie was born. The spa day sounds wonderful, but I really just want some alone time with you," Tess selfishly admitted.

"And you want to leave Mattie here?"

"My mom has offered to watch her. You know she would love it," she tried to persuade him.

He desperately wanted to make Tess happy. She had scarified so much to have this baby and the very least he could do was grant her this wish. "I'll talk to Fiona—see if she still wants me to scope out some leads. She did mention interest in opening a gallery in London."

"Oh, wouldn't that be great if she did? Maybe we could move to England."

"What about NYU? You've got two more years to go."

"I could transfer and finish my degree over there. I never did get to study abroad like I wanted," she reminded him.

"But what about your mother? She won't be able to see Mattie. And we won't have Alice on standby either." Sebastian paused for a moment than added, "I thought you were looking forward to an internship next summer. I'm not sure you'd qualify if we move to England now."

"Damn, you're right," Tess said, disappointed.

"Who can say what the future holds," Sebastian said in an effort to raise her spirits. "Stranger things have happened."

* * *

Tess had never been to a spa before and was taken aback when she entered the tranquil space. The lighting was soft, and soothing instrumental music played in the background, sounding like Oriental instruments and a babbling brook. She was given a plush terry robe and slippers to change into, and then she was guided to a tranquility room. Taking a seat in a velvet-covered lounge chair, she was offered spring water with a slice of fresh lemon, which she happily accepted. Then she opened her book and read until it was time for her treatment.

Fifteen minutes later she was taken into a private room for her massage. Lying on her stomach, Tess felt the therapist began to rub her back in a circular motion. The smell of lavender filled the room and Tess inhaled the wonderful scent. As the ninety-minute session continued, Tess felt the tension in her body melt away. It almost felt as if her mind had disconnected from her body and she was floating. This was one time she didn't mind Sebastian's extravagance; in fact, he was going to get a big thank you for this later.

After the massage, she was treated to an apricot facial and then a delicious lunch in the café. In the afternoon, Tess relaxed in the heated whirlpool, read her novel, and then sat down in the beautician's chair to have her hair and makeup done.

Looking in the mirror at her reflection after the beautician was finished, Tess hardly recognized herself. Her hair was cut and blow-dried straight, the added highlights catching the light. Her complexion was glowing—she felt like a new person. She felt beautiful.

Tess arrived home at four o'clock. It was unusually quiet; Sebastian and Mattie were nowhere in sight. She looked in the bedrooms first, but they were empty. She kicked off her shoes and padded into the living room. There, sprawled out on the couch, lay Sebastian with Mattie nestled on top of him, sleeping peacefully. Watching them brought a smile to her face. Sebastian's deep breaths made Mattie rise and fall on his chest, her small fist clutching her father's navy polo shirt, her mouth open with a little string of drool leaving a mark on his shirt. Tess had never seen anything so sweet or sexy in her entire life.

She slowly approached her sleeping family and gently pulled Mattie from Sebastian's chest. It woke him with a start. "Shh, I didn't mean to wake you," she whispered to her husband. "I'll just put Mattie in her crib."

Sebastian stood, stretching tall, his arms over his head and his bare abs peeking out as the polo rode up his stomach. He sauntered into his daughter's room behind Tess, who laid Mattie on the mattress in the crib. Placing a cotton blanket over the infant, she rubbed Mattie's back. The infant remained asleep, blissfully unaware.

Sebastian curled his arms around Tess and kissed her on the neck. Whenever he kissed her there, a jolt of desire rushed right to her center. She turned around and eyed him up. His hair was mussed, polo shirt was untucked; the top button of his jeans was undone and he wasn't wearing a belt.

"Welcome home," he whispered. "Did you enjoy your day at the spa?"

Tess took him by the hand and lead him out of Mattie's room, closing the door behind them with a soft click. A wicked smile formed on her face as she grabbed him by the belt loops and pulled him into their bedroom. She kissed him with passion, her hot tongue melding with his.

"Mrs. Irons, what is it that has you so aroused today?" Sebastian playfully questioned as he untied the belt on her wrap dress.

"You're so damn sexy," she muttered between kisses, pulling the polo over his head. The tips of her fingers traced the hard, sculpted plane of his chest, making their way down his abs, tracing the light trail of wiry hair that started at his navel and disappeared under his boxers.

Sebastian frantically stepped out of his jeans and boxers, his erection springing free. He slipped the dress off her shoulders and let it fall onto the floor. Standing back, he admired her body.

Tess stood there in her bra and panties while Sebastian's eyes ravished her. She enjoyed the view of his naked body and licked her lips at the thought of what would come next.

"God, you're so beautiful, it hurts," Sebastian muttered, taking a quick step toward Tess and enveloping her in his arms. He trailed urgent kisses along her neck and down to her cleavage. Cupping her breasts, he squeezed them and felt her nipples pebble under the light blue lace.

"Make love to me, Bas."

Oh, I plan on it, Sebastian thought to himself as he flicked the clasp of her bra open and pulled the bra off. Slowly, he pushed her backwards and laid her on the bed. Sebastian continued to kiss her luscious mouth while his hands explored her naked body. He missed this closeness with his wife. A part of his mind wanted to take it slow and savor her like a fine wine, while the other part wanted to bury himself deep inside her and never leave.

He grabbed a condom from the bedside drawer and stood up to roll it on.

"Let me do it," Tess said as she swung her legs over the side of the bed and sat up to face him.

He handed her the foil packet, but instead of ripping it open, Tess laid it on the bed next to her. Her lips curled up in to a smile as she eyed his cock. Before he could utter a word, her lips were caressing the head, and then she took him into her mouth. Sebastian reached out and grabbed her shoulders for support. Closing his eyes, he leaned back on his heels and enjoyed the heat of her mouth and the movement of her tongue.

"Darling, I'm not going to be able to make love you to if you keep this up," he choked out in a husky voice.

Tess pulled back and Sebastian's breath hissed through his gritted teeth. She tore the foil packet open and rolled the latex over his erection. Next she slipped off her panties and laid back on the bed.

Sebastian was through with foreplay. He need to be inside her now. Spreading her legs, he nestled himself between her thighs and slipped inside her. Sebastian's movements were slow and deliberate. Hovering above her body, looking into her eyes, he said, "You feel like heaven."

His declaration brought Tess to tears. "I love you," she whispered, overcome with emotion.

"I love you, too," he said as he quickened the pace of his thrust and climaxed with a shudder.

Panting, he withdrew from Tess and disposed of the condom. Then he was on his knees, creeping toward her, scattering little kisses along the delicate skin of her inner thighs. Next his tongue flicked her clit and she arched her back to meet his eager tongue. When he slipped his finger inside, she let out a quick gasp. Sebastian coaxed her to orgasm and knew he had accomplished his mission when her body eased back into the mattress and a wistful breath escaped her lips.

Sebastian curled around Tess' body, laying his head on her breast. "Oh how I've missed being with you like this."

"Yes," Tess said, as she absentmindedly ran her fingers through his hair. "I'm so relaxed, I could just fall asleep," she added as a yawn escaped her lips.

Just then the baby began to cry. "You stay here and rest. I'll fetch her," Sebastian said as he untangled himself from Tess. He stood and slipped on his boxers.

"No, I'll come with you," Tess told him, as she too got up from the bed and grabbed her robe.

They walked into Mattie's room together. Tess reached into the crib and picked up her daughter.

After locating the pacifier, Tess put it in the infant's mouth. The cries subsided as Mattie began to suck.

Sebastian slid his arm around Tess' waist and smiled at the scene in front of him. "I fall more in love with my girls every day," he said as he leaned down and kissed his wife. Mattie wrapped her hand around his finger and Sebastian was filled with joy.

Epilogue

Summer 1991 - Four years later

Tess walked into the condo to the smell of chicken roasting in the oven. She found Sebastian sitting on the sofa with Mattie, reading a children's book. "Hey, you two," she greeted, dropping her briefcase on the floor.

"Mummy!" Mattie exclaimed, jumping off the couch and running to hug her mom.

"How was your day?" she asked, kneeling down to Mattie's eye level.

"Great! Daddy is teaching me to read."

"I hope he's starting you out with something good."

Sebastian walked over and kissed Tess on the cheek. "Just something light—*War and Peace*."

Tess laughed aloud while Mattie cocked her head and gave her a confused look. "What's so funny?" the child asked.

"Daddy made a joke."

"It wasn't funny," Mattie replied. She ran back to the sofa and grabbed her book. She picked it up to show Tess the cover. It was Dr. Seuss' *One Fish, Two Fish, Red Fish, Blue Fish.*

"You're starting her off with poetry?"

"Well, it's not Keats."

"She's four years old, Bas. Cut her some slack," Tess chided.

"Ah, this from the valedictorian of St. Alexander's High School and graduate of NYU with honors."

"I'm going to change," Tess said, ignoring his comment.

"Dinner will be ready in fifteen minutes." Sebastian turned to his daughter. "Mattie, go wash your hands before we eat."

After dinner, they tucked Mattie into bed and Sebastian read her a bedtime story: *A Bear Called Paddington.* At least he tried to read her the story, but Mattie kept interrupting.

"Do bears really like marmalade?" she asked.

"I don't see why not. The next time I run into one, I'll ask him."

Mattie giggled. "Daddy, where are you going to run into a bear in New York?"

"The Central Park Zoo."

"Oh, yeah," Mattie agreed nodding her head.

"Your daddy used to live in London a long time ago," Tess added.

"Have you been to Paddington Station?" Mattie asked, her eyes wide with excitement.

"Yes, I have."

"I want to go! Maybe we can find Paddington Bear there."

Sebastian glanced over at Tess with a look that said *see what you started?* Tess simply smiled and took a seat in Sebastian's lap. "I want to go, too," she chimed in.

"Enough for tonight—time for bed." He closed the book and set it on Mattie's bedside table. Then he leaned over and kissed his little girl. "Love you, darling."

"'Night, Mattie," Tess said, also giving her daughter a kiss.

Sebastian turned off the light. He and Tess left the room before he closed the bedroom door.

It was blissfully quiet once Mattie fell to sleep. Sebastian and Tess curled up on the couch together, enjoying some time alone. Since graduating NYU, Tess had gotten a job with the Associated Press. Sebastian continued working at Fiona Ashford Gallery in Chelsea on a part-time basis while raising Mattie. They had settled into a happy, calm existence. It was a welcome change of pace for the couple. The first few years living together had certainly been bumpy, but they'd survived and become stronger people for it. Now they both had everything they'd ever wanted.

"Sooooo…I have some big news," Tess announced, looking up at her husband.

"What?"

"The AP offered me a position in London!" Tess said, bursting with excitement.

"Really? So soon? You've only worked there for a few years."

"I know, but I was talking with my boss. I told him that you're English and you keep up on the current news trends going on over there. He thought I'd be the perfect person for the position."

"Because you have an 'in' with me?" Sebastian chuckled. "See, I told you it's always who you know that matters in life. I just never thought I'd be talking about myself."

"I don't care if you were the one that tipped the job in my favor, I want to do it. What do you think? Can we move to London?"

Sebastian held Tess in his arms and pondered what she had just asked of him. He knew it was a dream of his wife's to travel the world and work as a journalist. He couldn't deny her the opportunity. He was just surprised that it was London and not some other European city. Sebastian did miss his homeland, and he thought of all the fun he could have showing his daughter around town. "I say we do it."

Tess gave him a big, toothy grin. "Thank you! I love you!"

"When do they want you to move?"

"In a month. I told them I would need to make a trip over to find a place to live first. I had a video conference with the London office and they said they'd help us set everything up. Just imagine—we'll be able to see Penny and Sigourney more often." Sigourney had moved back to London for a position in the London Symphony Orchestra, and he did miss being able to see her.

"Then I'll book the tickets. Mattie's going to love this!"

Want to find out what happens next?
Follow Sebastian, Tess and Mattie on their adventure in
London Loves - Love's Great Adventure Series - Book 3
coming Fall 2014.

About the Author

Theresa Troutman lives in Pennsylvania with her husband and their crazy dog, Niko. She loves reading, theatre, traveling, finding new authors to love, and her amazing friends.

Other titles by Theresa Troutman:

My Secret Summer
A Special Connection
Life's What You Make it
London Loves:
Love's Great Adventure Series Book 3 will be released
Fall 2014.

Connect with Theresa:

https://www.facebook.com/theresa.troutman.author
Twitter: @ theresatroutman
https://plus.google.com/u/0/115668965539628278155/posts
http://www.pinterest.com/theresa4503/

Looking to keep up with the latest news, excerpts and deleted scenes? Sign up for my newsletter.

website:
http://theresatroutman.wix.com/theresa-troutman

An excerpt from
A Special Connection

Chapter 1

I was trying to hurry to my class, but my stupid leg wouldn't cooperate. Even after all the physical therapy and hard work, I would forever have a limp—definitely not sexy to the girls or manly enough for the guys. I made it to class just as the professor began his lecture. My professors never gave me any problems due to my 'disability' and I always sat in the front row of every class so I didn't have to hobble very far. Slumping into the chair, I grabbed my notebook from my backpack.

College life was so different from high school. In high school I was laughed at and ridiculed. My life sucked. I was the resident cripple boy. Now, people didn't seem to pay any attention to me. It went from one extreme to another. I had to admit, this new phase of my life took some getting used to.

I opened my notebook. There was a small cartoon doodle of three stick figures: a boy, a girl, and a boy with a squiggle leg. All of their arms were interlinked. I'd know Samantha's handiwork anywhere. She had a brilliant mind, but she'd never make a go of it as an artist. She had written, *Meet you in the library at 3:00. Love you! Samantha.*

I loved Samantha Andrews. She was one of my best friends. It wasn't a sexual love, but something much deeper, I think. I was an eighteen-year-old virgin and had never kissed a girl. What did I know? We met freshman year of high school. Sam was the only girl who could look me in the eye and talk to me. She wasn't like the other girls, who would make comments about me behind my back and avoid my glances. She was wicked smart, which was a huge help to me because she became my study partner. Thanks to Sam, my grades were good. I couldn't imagine my life without her.

My other best friend was Rick Welsh. He lived next door to my granddad's house and I met him after the accident. Rick was the star basketball player on our high school's team. At six-foot five, with blond hair, ripped muscles, and a charming grin, he was every girl's dream and every guy's envy. We were an unlikely pair; the kid that could run and jump with finesse and ease was partnered with the limping slowpoke. The thing that sealed the deal for me and made us lifelong friends was the day Rick defended me against a bully who tripped me in the hall my freshman year. Rick was one of the cool kids and I'm sure he took some flak for standing up for me, but no one ever physically touched me after that incident. And for that I have Rick to thank.

I made my way over to the round table by the window in the library. Sam and Rick were already seated, the picture of a perfect couple. They'd been dating for a little more than a year. When they first got together, I felt very awkward about it, but did my best to hide my feelings. These two people meant the world to me and I didn't want to lose their friendship due to a bout of jealousy.

"Hi," I greeted, taking a seat next to Sam. She was wearing a form-fitting, white polo shirt tucked into her belted black jeans. Her brunette hair fell over her shoulders. Sam had perfect hair, like a model in a shampoo commercial—perfectly straight, no frizz or flyaways.

"Jake, did you work on your essay last night? I could take a look at it for you," Sam offered.

"I could use your help," I admitted. I pulled my laptop out of my bag and turned it on. Once I'd opened my file, I slid the computer towards Sam. She began reading at once.

"You're not going to miss my game, are you?" Rick asked.

"No, Richard," Samantha said, sounding like a tired old housewife. "Jake and I will be there for the game."

I chuckled. "I don't know, Rick. You've seen one basketball game, you've seen them all."

"Hey, there will be an NBA scout coming to watch the game tonight! You two are my good luck charms."

"You can't possibly expect the scout to pick you out of all the players."

"Gee, Sam, thanks for the support."

"I'm just being realistic. You should stay in school and get your degree. You're on a scholarship and you should take advantage of that. You'll be glad you did when your NBA career is over," Sam said.

"Well, at least you believe I can have an NBA career."

"Of course I do." Sam leaned in and kissed Rick on the cheek. "You're an amazing player. I believe if you work hard, you can get drafted."

Her remark lightened Rick's mood. I was happy to avoid being caught in the middle of one of their arguments.

"I gotta go," Rick said. "I'll see you both tonight."

Sam watched Rick as he exited the library. "Thanks for playing nice," I remarked.

"No point in fighting with him now, only to ruin his game."

"You're a wise woman, Sam."

"Yes, I know."

"And very humble," I teased.

"I can't help it that I'm usually right," she said with a wicked grin.

"I'm going home after we finish here. I promised Jenna I'd give her a lift to the game tonight." Jenna was Rick's younger sister. She was seventeen and in her senior year of high school. The Welshes lived next door to me and my granddad, so it was no big deal to have her tag along.

"Great. It will be good to see her."

The gymnasium was filled to capacity. There was a buzz of excitement emanating through the crowd. They were psyched that it was Friday and the Villanova Wildcats were playing their rival, Georgetown. The bleachers were a sea of blue and white. People were holding banners and pom-poms, geared up for a showdown. I sat between Sam and Jenna. Sam was holding onto my hand so tightly it had become numb. I don't know what type of drug

Rick was taking, but I wanted some, too. He was on: flawless, strong, and energetic. I wished I knew how that felt. I longed for the gazes of admiration that came with being a star athlete.

"Samantha, I'm losing feeling in my hand," I gently whispered in her ear as she watched Rick bound down the court with great intensity.

When my words finally sunk into her brain, she released my hand. "I'm sorry, Jake. God, I'm so nervous for him."

"He's having the game of his life. If that scout is watching, he'll certainly leave a lasting impression."

She looked at me and smiled. "I hope you're right."

The clock began to count down the final seconds and Rick was in possession of the ball. He poised for the three-point shot.

"He'll never make it," Sam said.

"Just watch," I responded as the ball sailed through the air and hit the rim of the basket, tipping into the net. Rick did it! Our team won the game.

The crowd roared to life. Pandemonium ensued as fans rushed the court. Sam jumped up and down on the bleachers, screaming her excitement. The next thing I knew, she was in my arms. In that moment, I swear time stopped. Sam and I had a platonic friendship; I didn't understand why I was feeling an odd flutter in my gut. Then she kissed me on the lips. It was just a quick, friendly kiss, but it surprised me. I sucked in a breath. Before I could say anything, Samantha was passing me and running down to the court to congratulate Rick.

Maybe it was best she'd left me. What could I possibly say to her? Jenna stood next to me. She silently put her hand on my shoulder and gave a faint smile. We sat together in silence, waiting for the rest of the people to leave the stands so I could hobble down alone and undetected once the gym was empty.